THE COMPLETE CASES
OF JIM BENNETT

OTHER BOOKS IN THE DIME DETECTIVE UNIFORM EDITION LIBRARY:

The Complete Cases of Carter Cole, Volume 1 by Frederick C. Davis

The Complete Cases of Doc Pierce, Volume 1 by Richard Dermody

The Complete Cases of Johnny Cass by Roger D. Torrey

The Complete Cases of Max Latin by Norbert Davis

The Complete Cases of Needle Mike, Volume 2 by William E. Barrett

THE COMPLETE CASES OF JIM BENNETT™

VOLUME 1

ROBERT MARTIN

ILLUSTRATIONS BY

FRANK KRAMER

V.E. PYLES

POPULAR PUBLICATIONS • 2022

First Edition—2022

PUBLISHING HISTORY

"GI Doublecross" originally appeared in the March 1945 issue of *Dime Detective* magazine. Copyright 1945 by Popular Publications, Inc. Copyright renewed 1973 and assigned to Steeger Properties, LLC. All rights reserved.

"Murder Without Music" originally appeared in the August 1945 issue of *Thrilling Detective* magazine. Copyright 1945 by Standard Magazines, Inc.

"Killers Can't Be Careless" originally appeared in the November 1946 issue of *Dime Detective* magazine. Copyright 1946 by Popular Publications, Inc. Copyright renewed 1974 and assigned to Steeger Properties, LLC. All rights reserved.

"Nice, Like a Cobra" originally appeared in the February 1947 issue of *Thrilling Detective* magazine. Copyright 1947 by Standard Magazines, Inc.

TABLE OF CONTENTS

GI DOUBLECROSS

IT WAS GETTING TO BE A HABIT. TWICE IN TWELVE HOURS I HAD TAKEN THE COUNT, AND ALL BECAUSE THE BOSS HAD SAID: "GET TO THAT GIRL AND KEEP AFTER HER. FIND OUT ABOUT HER BROTHER!" BUT JAKE ALLEN WAS DEAD—KILLED IN A PLANE CRASH, SO THE PAPERS SAID, AND STILL "ACCIDENTS" WERE OCCURRING IN KEY WAR PLANTS—"ACCIDENTS" WHICH DISABLED AND KILLED HUNDREDS OF INNOCENT WORKERS AND EFFECTIVELY CRIPPLED THE COUNTRY'S AIRPLANE PRODUCTION.

CHAPTER ONE
START THE BALL ROLLING

IT WAS about five o'clock in the afternoon when I got out of the taxi in front of the Club Americana. I paid the driver and stood on the sidewalk, looking the place over.

It was just another club, maybe a little better than most, with the usual big, colored photographs of the current band leader and the floor show attractions. The girl's picture was there, too—blond, brown eyes, a nice smile. Beneath her picture were the words: *Judy Allen, Mistress of Song.* She looked O.K., but not what I had expected. The boss hadn't told me much about her, except that she was singing at the Americana. I had expected her to appear glittery, hard-looking. But she looked nice.

I went inside, checked my hat and coat, and a waiter led me to a table along a wall. I said: "Thanks, I'll sit at the bar."

I sat on a stool and ordered a double Manhattan. "I'll have at least two," I told the pretty girl tending bar. "You may as well make them both at once."

She smiled, began pouring vermouth into a stirring glass. I watched her add the whiskey and bitters, and then I looked around the room. The cocktail crowd was gathering fast, and the place was humming with conversation and filled with the pleasant smell of liquor and lemons. There were a lot of men in uniform, both Army and Navy.

I was a little envious of them, and suddenly very conscious of my civilian tweeds.

I turned back to the bar. An oversized cocktail glass sat in front of me, with two cherries reposing in its clear amber depths. I tasted the drink. "Very good," I told the girl behind the bar. "Just the right amount of bitters."

She smiled, said, "Thank you," and began to measure gin into a shaker. I asked her when the band began playing, and she said: "Five-thirty."

I looked at my watch. Five-twenty. So I sipped my drink and watched the crowd. Pretty soon the musicians came out and took their places on the raised platform at the end of the long, narrow room. At precisely five-thirty they began to play. The music was good, soft and low. The small

dance floor was soon jammed. I watched and waited.

At the end of the second number she came out, looking, under the lights, even prettier than her picture. She came out smiling and stood in front of the microphone. Everyone clapped. I set down my glass and clapped, too.

They turned a blue spot on her and she began to sing. She was O.K. She had a low, pleasing voice, and while she was singing no one talked. Everyone listened.

I thought: Well, there she is. Time to get to work.

I finished my drink, laid some money on the bar, and asked a passing waiter if he could get me a table. He led me over next to the wall and put me down at a small table for two jammed between larger tables. It was still too early to eat, so I ordered another Manhattan. When the waiter brought it, I slipped a buck into his ready hand. "Look," I said, "could I speak to Miss Allen?"

The waiter was an old guy with white hair. He smiled, said, "I'll see, sir," and went away.

When she finished singing I saw him go up and speak to her, and he looked toward my table. She looked, too, and I smiled at her. She did not smile at me. She merely shook her head at the waiter, sat down in a chair beside the second sax player, folded her hands in her lap, and looked primly out across the dance floor.

The waiter came back. "I'm sorry, sir," he said. He really looked sorry.

I said: "That's all right. Thanks."

The waiter went away, and I took another swallow of my drink and tried to figure out another approach. I had to talk to her, but I also had to be careful.

A voice behind me said: "Tough luck."

I TURNED around in my chair. At a small table behind me sat a lone soldier. On his sleeve were a sergeant's chevrons. Above his left breast pocket were Army Air Force wings and a service ribbon. He was drinking a bottle of beer, and he grinned at me.

"Sergeant," I said, "you have sharp ears. Will you have a drink?"

He said, "Sure," picked up his beer and his glass and moved over to my table. "I don't blame you for trying," he said. "She's all right."

"Do you know her?" I asked.

"No," he replied, "but I'd like to. Want me to try?"

"Sure," I said. "Go ahead."

He turned in his chair to motion to the waiter, but at that moment the band began to play. The girl stood up in front of the microphone to sing again. The sergeant turned back to the table. "Too late now," he said. "Have to wait until she finishes."

I ordered beer for him, and another Manhattan for myself. "South Pacific, I see," I said, motioning to his service ribbon.

He said: "Yeah. First leave in a year. Gotta go back next week."

He told me a little about himself. He said his name was Dan Malloy, and that he was a waist-gunner on a B-17. His folks were dead. All by himself on furlough, and no place to go. Said he had some relatives in Cleveland, Ohio, but that it was too far from San Francisco, and he guessed he would just hang around until time to go back.

He didn't ask me any questions, and I didn't tell him much. I get tired of making up stories to tell people, and I like people who don't ask questions. I did tell him that my name was Jim Bennett, that I was from New York, which was true, and that I was out on the coast on business, which was also true. I didn't tell him what kind of business.

Pretty soon the girl finished her song, and Sergeant Malloy asked the waiter if he could speak to Miss Allen.

The waiter glanced at me and smiled faintly. "I'll see, sir," he said again, and went away.

We both watched him. When he spoke to the girl, she looked again at our table. The sergeant raised his hand, and grinned at her. She didn't look at me, but she smiled at him a little uncertainly. The waiter said something to her, she nodded and gathered the skirt of her long black dress in her hand. Then she stepped down from the platform, walked around the edge of the dance floor, and came up to our table. The sergeant winked at me, and we both stood up.

The sergeant held a chair for her. "Thanks for coming, Miss Allen," he said, very politely. "My name is Dan Malloy. This gentleman is Mr. Bennett, of New York."

Her cool gaze flicked over me, and back to Malloy. She sat down in the chair he was holding for her, said: "Thank you, Sergeant."

I said: "Miss Allen, would you care for a drink?"

She glanced at me briefly, said, "No, thanks," and turned to the sergeant.

He said: "I wanted to tell you how much I enjoyed your singing."

"Thank you," she said. "I'm glad you liked it."

It was just small talk, conventional talk. Maybe she figured it was part of her job to be nice to the boys in uniform. But I had a job to do. I liked the sergeant, and I was grateful for his help in getting her to the table. It was the first step in a tough job, and I didn't want any slips. The boss had been very blunt about it, as usual. "Get to the girl," he had said. "Find out about her brother. We know that Jake Allen was involved in the blasting of tunnel kilns in war plants making grinding wheels for the aircraft industry—and without grinding wheels not an airplane could be built, nor a ship, nor a tank, nor a gun, for that matter.

Find out where Jake Allen is, and what he's doing now. Get the goods on him. Prove it. Stop him!"

"It must be the uniform," I said to Judy Allen.

She stopped her conversation with the sergeant long enough to notice me. "It must be," she said.

I was certainly getting off to a fine friendly start.

WHILE SHE was talking to the sergeant, I ran over in my mind the things the boss had told me about Jake Allen. It wasn't too much, but we were pretty certain that he had been responsible for the almost total loss of a plant in Ohio, and another in New York State. Then we got a tip that he was moving west. His game was always the same. He would get work in grinding wheel factories under various names. Considering the manpower shortage it wasn't hard for him to get a job. Employers were too hard up for men, especially men with a 4-F draft classification, to bother to check them too carefully.

As near as we could find out, Jake Allen claimed to have had experience in the operation of kilns, and got work in the kiln departments. A two hundred foot tunnel kiln loaded with vital abrasive wheels destined to grind the precision parts of bomber motors was his meat. On his last job he had apparently placed a time bomb on one of the cars moving slowly through the tunnel kiln. The bomb had been set to explode at the very center of the kiln, the spot where the gas—or oil—generated heat was the most intense. The explosion had not only wrecked the kiln and thousands of dollars' worth of precious grinding wheels nearing completion, but a good portion of the plant as well. Also, it had killed six men, and injured a number of others. Meanwhile, the plant's production was very effectively stopped, and one bomber plant was shut down until other grinding wheels could be rushed to it.

That was the kind of thing happening all over the country. Sometimes it would be a time bomb or stick of dynamite attached to a time clock which would explode when an employee punched his card. Outwardly, they were just unfortunate accidents, just those inevitable things which are always occurring in times of boom production. Sometimes they were, but not always. Pretty often they were not accidents. To too many people the word "sabotage" is just another bad radio joke, but men in my work know better. A couple of the boys had come up with some dope on Jake Allen, and it looked bad. After his last job he had dropped out of sight. Then they found out some more—that he done a stretch in the pen, which accounted for the 4-F, and that he had a sister in San Francisco. I had just come off a west coast shipyard job, and the boss put me on Allen's trail. And here I was sitting at a table with Jake Allen's sister and twiddling my thumbs while she talked to Sergeant Malloy.

They were having quite a conversation—all about his experiences in the Pacific. "Excuse me," I said, "would you like a drink?"

The sergeant said: "Sure. Another beer." I looked at the girl, and her gaze flicked cooly over me. "Nothing, thank you," she said. "I go on again in a few minutes."

"That's all right," said the sergeant. "We'll save it for you."

She smiled at him. "No, really," she said, and got to her feet.

Malloy and I both stood up. I was thinking fast. "Miss Allen," I said, "I really did want to speak with you."

"Yes?" she said.

Suddenly there was a man standing behind her. He was in uniform, too, and I saw the gleam of the two silver bars on his shoulder. Malloy saluted smartly, and the newcomer returned it casually. He was looking at the girl. "Judy," he said, "how are you?"

She turned. "Why, Captain Smythe."

Smythe, I thought. Captain John Smythe, I presume? And how is Pocahontas?

The captain took her hand. She turned to the sergeant, said: "Captain Smythe, this is Sergeant Dan Malloy."

The captain nodded, and looked at me. "And Mr. Bennett," she said.

I held out my hand. He hesitated for a second, then took it in a limp grasp. "Pleased, Captain Smith," I said.

A slight frown crossed his handsome features. "Smythe," he said—" 'y' like in 'eye.' "

"Sorry," I said. "Won't you sit down?"

We all sat down, and I thought that it was getting to be quite a party. But I didn't care—at least it kept the girl at the table for a little longer. But it didn't do me much good. She talked to the captain and the sergeant and seldom looked at me. After a while the captain began talking about dinner, and that was all right with me. I was beginning to get hungry. So the waiter came, and we all ordered. Judy Allen left the table several times to sing, but she always came back. I figured I had the captain to thank for that. During one of the times when she was gone, he said: "Mr. Bennett, what is your business?"

"Grinding wheels," I said.

"Oh," he replied. "You mean emery stones?"

I had been reading up on abrasives since the boss had put me on Allen's trail. "No," I said. "I mean grinding wheels."

"What's the difference?"

"Plenty," I said. "Emery stone is an obsolete expression used fifty years ago, like we used to say horseless carriage for automobile. Modern grinding wheels are not stones. They are a highly scientific product composed of bauxite, silicon carbide and other agents, very delicately fused and blended, and burned in ovens, round or tunnel-type kilns at a temperature of—"

"Really?" the captain broke in. "Very interesting." He turned to the sergeant. "Sergeant, how is your fish?"

"Very good, sir," said Malloy. Since the captain had joined our gay little group Sergeant Malloy had become visibly subdued.

Judy Allen came back to the table. I beat the captain by a split second and held her chair for her. We all sat down again, and I said: "Captain, in what branch of the service are you?"

Before he could answer, Judy Allen said: "Captain Smythe is a producer and writer of plays for the soldiers. He travels all over the country putting on educational shows for them. Don't you, Captain?"

"That's about it," he said. "Put on a show in Texas last week. Don't know where they'll send me next. Taking a little furlough now. I need it."

"I'll bet," I said. "It must be very strenuous. You and Sergeant Malloy have a lot in common."

I was immediately sorry I had said it. I really had nothing against him, and I knew well enough that every branch of the Service was important. Every man to his own job, where he can do the most good, myself included. But something about Captain Smythe irritated me. Maybe it was the way he spelled his name. Anyhow, I was sorry. Sergeant Malloy choked on a hunk of fish, and Judy Allen looked at me with an expression of distaste. The captain put down his knife and fork and touched a napkin to his lips. There was a silence for a few seconds. It was very awkward.

Judy Allen spoke. She said: "I've been wondering all evening. It's a rather personal question, I know, but what do you do, Mr. Bennett?" Her voice was as cold as ice.

The three of them were watching me, and there was no friendliness in their eyes. Even Sergeant Malloy looked reproachful. I said: "As I told the captain a while ago, my business is grinding wheels. Grinding wheels, you know, are extremely important to the war effort. Not a ship, or a plane, or a tank could be built without them." I reeled it off just the way I had read it.

"I see," said Captain Smythe. "On deferment?"

"No," I said. "Not exactly. Occupational classification in an essential industry."

The captain and sergeant said nothing. Judy Allen said: "Oh."

"You see, Miss Allen," I said, throwing out my first hook, "your brother and I have something in common. I understand that he is an abrasive worker, too."

Judy Allen said: "My brother is dead."

CHAPTER TWO
BROWN SHOE

THAT STOPPED me. All this build-up, and the guy I was looking for was dead! If Jake Allen had been blasting war factories, he apparently wasn't going to blast any more. It looked as though the boss's tip had certainly been cold.

"I'm very sorry," I said.

She was looking at her plate, and I thought I saw her lips tremble. And I suddenly thought how clean and bright her blond hair looked. Captain Smythe had taken her hand, and now he glared across the table at me. "You ought to be sorry," he said.

"Look," I said, "how did I know? I said I was sorry."

Besides being sorry, I wanted to know how and when, and all about it, but it wasn't the time or the place to question Judy Allen. I decided to stick around as long as I could. But the captain had other ideas.

"Mr. Bennett," he said, "I believe that Miss Allen would like to be alone. Do you mind?"

I minded, all right, and I wasn't going to be shooed away. After all, it was my table, and so far I was paying the bill. I looked at Sergeant Malloy, who hadn't said a word since Judy Allen's announcement of her brother's death.

He looked embarrassed. "Sergeant," I asked, "have you finished your dinner?"

The sergeant looked down at his still half-filled plate. But he did not hesitate. The captain's silver bars carried a lot of weight with him. He got to his feet. "All finished," he said, and looked expectantly at me.

I sat still. "Finish your dinner," I said. "I'm sure Miss Allen won't mind."

He hesitated, watching the captain. Judy Allen raised her head and smiled. It was a nice smile, sort of a through-the-tears smile. "Surely not, Sergeant," she said. "Please don't leave. Besides, it's time for me to go on again." She fished a tiny bit of lace from her bag and dabbed at her eyes. I was afraid her mascara would run, but it didn't. She got to her feet, and I beat the captain again by standing up first. But he took her arm and guided her through the crowd to the platform. She did not look back. Sergeant Malloy and I sat down.

"Too bad about her brother," he remarked.

"Yeah," I said. "The captain acts like an old friend. Is he?"

Malloy shrugged. "I don't know. He was with her last night."

"Here?" I asked.

"No. At a place uptown. In the bar of the Golden Gate Hotel."

"Oh," I said. "No wonder she came over to our table. You've met her."

He laughed. He had even white teeth. "No, not at all. I saw her, but she didn't notice me. I found out that she sang here, so here I am."

"To hear her sing?"

He grinned at me. "Sure," he said.

"I don't blame you," I said. "Like some more beer?"

"Sure," he said. Suddenly he got to his feet. I looked up. Captain Smythe was standing at our table.

"Sit down, Captain," I said. "Your fish is getting cold."

He sat, and so did the sergeant. But the captain didn't start to eat. He looked at me. His face was red. Behind us the orchestra began to play. The captain started to say something, but I couldn't hear him because of the music. I leaned toward him. I was close enough to smell the fancy shaving lotion on his handsome face.

"Bennett, you were pretty rude to Miss Allen."

The music grew softer just before Judy Allen began to sing. I leaned back in my chair, fished in my pocket for a cigarette. "How?" I asked.

"By arguing with me after she told you about her brother. She is naturally quite broken up over it. It happened only a week ago."

"You seem to know Miss Allen pretty well."

"Yes. Pretty well."

I didn't like the way he said it, but I thought, What the hell! Why shouldn't I like it? I said: "What happened to her brother?"

She had begun to sing, and the room had quieted down. The captain turned to look at her. "Airplane crash," he said, over his shoulder.

"When?" I asked. "Where?"

Slowly the captain turned in his chair. He looked at me for a long second. "Why?" he asked.

I shrugged. "Just curious."

"A week ago yesterday," he said. "Twenty miles out of Albuquerque. Great Western Airlines. At two-thirty-seven in the morning."

"Thanks," I said. "You seem to know all about it."

"Yes," he said.

I had read about the crash, but I didn't remember the name of Jake Allen on the list of victims. But then, when I had read about it, I hadn't been looking for Jake Allen. It could be.

"Bodies identified?" I asked.

"No," he replied. "Plane burned. Occupants identified by passenger list."

Sergeant Malloy sat listening to us. He hadn't said a word—just sat and listened and drank his beer. He looked bored. Judy Allen stopped singing, and the crowd applauded. The captain stood up and clapped his hands. She smiled across the room at him, but she did not return to our table. She sat down in her chair on the platform, and the captain left us and moved through the crowd toward her.

"Excuse me, Sergeant," I said. "I'll be back in a couple of minutes. Order me some coffee, will you?"

"Sure, Mr. Bennett," he said.

"Call me Jim."

"O.K., Jim." He grinned up at me.

I WENT out to the checkroom, found a phone booth, and called a private number in Los Angeles. As I slid quarters into the slot I thought that after being so nasty the captain had been pretty free with his information on the plane crash. In a couple of minutes I got my connection. George Baker answered. I could tell it was George by his cold-in-the-head voice.

"Listen, George," I said. "This is Bennett. Down in Frisco. Check that Great Western plane crash out of Albuquerque last week for me, will you? Passenger list, especially. Anything else you can get. Call me back. I'll wait." I gave him the number on the dial and hung up.

I stood in the doorway of the booth and smoked a cigarette. The dinner hour was about over, and people were leaving the Club Americana. Through the doorway I could see waiters already clearing tables for the evening trade. The music of the orchestra drifted out to me, but I could no longer hear the voice of Judy Allen. And then suddenly I saw her.

She came out of the doorway leading into the bar, and stood a moment looking about her. She looked scared. She had on a beaver coat over her evening dress. I figured I could hear the phone if I left the door open, so I walked over to her.

"Leaving, Miss Allen?" I asked, trying to smile in the approved play boy fashion.

It didn't go over. She didn't answer me, but kept looking around. She pulled her coat closer about her, and as she did so a small sequin bag dropped from her hand. I stooped to pick it up. It was heavy, and had a familiar feel. An automatic—about a .32, I guessed—is a big gun for such a little girl to carry. As I handed the bag to her, I thought: My, my, just like in the spy books—beautiful girl, gun in handbag, and everything. And then I heard Captain Smythe's voice.

"Judy, wait," he said.

I turned around. When the captain saw me, his eyes narrowed, and there was an unpleasant look about his mouth. He jerked me by the arm. "Get out of the way, Bennett," he said.

I had a notion to take a swing at him, uniform or no uniform. But the phone began ringing in the booth, and it kept ringing. I turned my back on them, and went into the booth. The captain and Judy Allen hurried to the street door, went outside, and stood on the sidewalk looking for a taxi. I could see them through the glass doors. She was standing very straight, and he held her by the arm. I took down the receiver, said, "Yeah," and George Baker's nasal, complaining voice came over the wire.

"Jim? Here's the dope. Great Western Airlines passenger plane crashed and burned on mountainside in heavy fog twenty-six miles north of Albuquerque at two-thirty-seven on the morning of the twenty-fourth. Cause of crash unknown. Experienced pilot, plane checked O.K. at Seattle before taking off. Pilot, co-pilot, twelve passengers burned beyond identification. Passenger list—you got it, Jim?"

"Yeah," I said. "Go ahead."

"Passenger list contained names of Albert Berstein, Russell C. Whitticker and wife, David L. Rockingham, Andrew Kelley, Jacob K. Allen—"

"Hold it, George," I said. "That's all. Thanks."

As I left the booth I saw that the captain and Judy Allen were gone. I stood for a minute, trying to decide what to do next. I remembered Sergeant Malloy, and I went back to the table. But the sergeant was gone, too.

Sergeant Malloy hadn't forgotten about my coffee. It was there on the table, but it was cold. I drank it anyway, and as I set the cup down, the white-haired waiter came up. I asked him for the check, and he said: "The soldier paid the bill, sir. He asked me to tell you that he was sorry he had to leave."

"O.K.," I said. "By the way, can you tell me where Miss Allen lives?"

"No, sir," he said, "I'm sorry."

I laid a five-spot on the table. He picked it up and put it in his pocket. As he leaned down to take my cup, he said: "Thank you, sir. Number 2614 Roycroft. Apartment 3-B."

"Thank you," I said, and went to get my hat and coat. The checkroom girl was pretty, and she smiled at me. I tossed a quarter in the dish with the rest of the decoy quarters, said, "Thanks," and went out.

It was dark outside, and the lights in front of the Club Americana were lit. They shone on the picture of Judy Allen, and something printed on the card attracted my attention. The words beneath her picture read: *Singing nightly—5:30 until 8:00; 10:00 until closing.*

I looked at my watch. Seven-twenty-five. She was leaving early. And I figured that if she had to be back at ten, she must not live very far away. Why go home at all? Surely, the Club Americana provided retiring rooms for its entertainers?

A taxi pulled up in front. I climbed in and gave the driver the address the waiter had given me. It wasn't far—eight blocks. Five straight north, and three east. We stopped in front of a medium-sized apartment building. I paid the taxi driver and went up the steps.

There was a lot of traffic in the street, and I didn't hear the shot. Maybe there was a silencer on the gun. Anyhow, as I pushed on the glass doors there was a sudden splintering sound beside my head and a jagged hole appeared in the glass of the door. Thin cracks, like the threads of a spiderweb, ran away from it. And I saw the quick puff of plaster dust from the wall inside.

I SLAMMED the door open, jumped inside, and flattened myself against the wall. I couldn't see anything outside but the traffic and the lights. Across the street there was a dark office building, and I figured that whoever had taken a crack at me could have hidden in the doorway. But he would have had to pick the right instant to clear the passing cars.

I waited a minute, but nothing else happened. I could see the names on the mail boxes on the other wall, and one of them contained a card which read: *Judy Allen, Apt. 3-B.* There was an elevator down the hall, but I waited another minute and then went up the stairs, two steps at a time. I got to the third floor and found apartment 3-B. I looked around for a place to duck, just in case, but there wasn't any. So I just stood in front of the door and listened.

It was quiet on this floor, and the traffic from down in the street was a low murmur. At first, I couldn't hear anything from inside the apartment. And then I heard voices, but I couldn't make out the words. I thought of the fire escape, walked down to the far end of the hall, and turned left. Sure, enough, there was a door at the end of the corridor. I opened it, and the cool night air struck my face. I went out onto the fire escape and looked along the wall of the building to about where I thought the windows of apartment 3-B would be. There was no way to get out there, but down past the windows ran a fire escape from two floors above. So I hot-footed it back inside, down the hall to the stairway and up to the fifth floor. I found the outside door and started down the fire escape. I got to a small landing at the third floor and did a little reconnaissance work. There was no ledge leading to the windows, but right behind me was a door. I tried it, and almost laughed out loud at my good luck. It was unlocked.

I pushed the door open carefully, and entered a dark room. As my eyes became accustomed to the gloom I saw that I was in a small kitchen, and there was a light shining under the far door. I tiptoed across to the door and opened it about a quarter of an inch. I could see Judy Allen, all right, but no one else. She was sitting in a chair by a window. She still had on the dress which she had worn at the club, and appeared to be alone—at least she wasn't talking or looking at anyone. I wondered what had become of Captain Smythe. I stood there maybe two or three minutes, just looking and listening.

The sudden jangling of the telephone almost made me jump. Judy Allen got up to answer it, and I hoped that her telephone was not in the kitchen. It wasn't, and I could hear her talking from somewhere out of my line of vision.

It was, naturally, a one-sided conversation for me. I heard her say: "Yes… Captain Smythe?… No I don't know—What?… Yes, yes, of course. Right away… yes, yes, yes."

I heard her replace the receiver, and for an instant she flitted across my line of vision. She was carrying her beaver coat, and she was almost running. The lights went off, and I heard a door slam. I waited a minute, and then I pushed open the kitchen door and entered the room.

The faint perfume of her presence was still there, and even in the dim light I could see that it was a nice room, furnished in good taste. I decided to risk turning on the lights, and found the wall switch. When the lights came on, I stood still for a minute, looking around.

There was a door at the far end, which I guessed entered into her bedroom, several chairs, a writing desk, a book case—lots of books in it, too—drapes at the windows, a thick rug the color of coffee with cream in it. On the desk were several photographs, and I moved over and looked at them. One was of a good-looking, black-haired, black-browed man in an open-necked sports shirt. Written across the bottom in heavy, inked letters were the words: *To Sis, with much love. Jake.*

There was another picture of two elderly, pleasant-faced people, apparently her parents, and one of a handsome boy with a black mustache and wavy black hair. On this picture was written: *To Judy, with all my love—Jeff.*

I looked at the picture of Jake Allen more closely. This was the guy who was suspected of blowing up two war plants, the guy I was trying to catch in the act. Well, he was dead, or supposed to be, and I was up a blind alley.

Something made me turn around. I don't know what caused me to turn—there was no sound. Maybe it was that back-of-the-neck feeling you have when someone is staring at you. The kitchen door was opening slowly. I grabbed for my .38, and in the same instant a hand came through the opening of the door. In the hand was a gun. The gun had an oversized barrel, which I knew to be a silencer—a scarce item these days.

I ducked down, and as my gun came out I heard a sharp spitting sound, a small stifled explosion. Even as I squeezed the trigger of my .38 and saw my slug strike splinters from the kitchen door I felt a sledge hammer blow on my head, and a searing, momentary pain. I went to my knees, and heard the choking explosion again. A small dark hole appeared in the rug beside my hand. I tried to raise my gun again, but I couldn't make it. I fell forward and saw the rug fly up to meet my face. The room swam in blackness, and I went out, cold.

But I remembered one thing before I passed out. On the wrist of the hand which held the gun behind the kitchen door there showed an inch of coat sleeve. The color of the coat sleeve was olive drab.

I WAS out maybe twenty minutes. Not really out, because I knew I was lying on the thick rug, and that my head was hurting—bad. But I couldn't get up. The lights were still on in the room, and I just laid there on my face and the events of the last few hours crawled across my brain in a slow, mixed-up way, over and over again.

After what seemed like a long time I heard a key in the door, and voices, but I couldn't move even then. Things were coming into a little sharper focus, but I didn't have enough strength to move a finger. And it didn't particularly bother me, except for the terrific pain in my head. I was perfectly content to stay where I was and let the world drift by. It was very strange.

A man's voice said: "Judy! What the hell—"

I opened my eyes and saw a big pair of brown shoes beside my face. One of the shoes lifted up and pushed my head sideways, not very gently. As my head twisted around I saw a pair of man's trousers. They were a dark gray color, and they were very neatly pressed. Beyond the pants and the brown shoes I saw the bottom of a floor-length black skirt and the toe of one small silver slipper.

Brown Shoe lifted his foot and my head rolled back again, as if it were on a rubber band. I closed my eyes again, but not before I had noticed the wet red smear on the rug beneath my face. My face was wet and sticky, and I knew it was blood, my own blood, but I didn't care. Nothing worried me. I just wanted the pain in my head to stop.

I heard the girl ask: "Is he dead?"

Another voice from above me—Brown Shoe's, I suppose—said: "I don't think so. Who is he? How did he get in here? Judy, what about it?"

She answered something, but I didn't get it. I was beginning to feel a little better. Things were starting to focus, and

I knew I was in a spot. I thought about trying to get to my feet, and I moved my legs. Brown Shoe kicked me in the side, not easy. I was far enough back to normal to get mad at that. I moved my legs again. They seemed to work O.K. I began to gather the muscles in my arms, was on the point of pushing myself upward, when Brown Shoe kicked me again. It hurt. I lay still for a minute, and in that minute I worked up a healthy hate for Brown Shoe, whoever he was.

Then I heard a swish of skirts, and the girl's voice saying: "Don't." Then the black skirt and the little silver slippers were right beside my face. I felt cold water on my head and face. It felt swell. I smelled the faint perfume which meant Judy Allen to me. She bathed my head and face, very gently, and I felt better by the second. I rolled over on my side and looked up into her face.

"Thanks," I said, surprised at the sound of my voice. It sounded far away, and very faint. I tried it again. "Thanks," I said, louder.

She said nothing. Behind her stood a big, black-haired man. He needed a shave, but otherwise he looked very neat and well-dressed in a dark gray double-breasted suit. Judy Allen continued to bathe my head. Her lips were pressed together in a tight straight line. Over her shoulder she said to Brown Shoe: "Call the police."

Brown Shoe didn't move. She turned back to me. "What are you doing here? What happened?"

I pushed myself to a sitting position, and for a couple of dizzy seconds I thought I would have to flop back again. But I made it. I saw my gun lying on the floor beside me. I reached for it, but Brown Shoe stepped up and kicked it out from under my fingers.

I looked at Judy Allen. "I'm sorry about your rug."

Without answering me, she looked up at Brown Shoe. "Call the police," she repeated.

"No hurry," he said. "What about this guy?"

"I told you. I met him at the club tonight. He mentioned knowing my brother."

Brown Shoe said: "Yeah. You told me that. But who is he?"

Judy Allen didn't answer. She got up and crossed to the telephone. I heard her ask for the police department, and then I heard her giving her address. I answered Brown Shoe's question. "Jim Bennett," I said.

"Shut up," he barked.

I felt mean. I said: "Who the hell are you?"

He started toward me, but from across the room the girl said: "No."

He stopped and looked down at me. He was a big guy. There was an ugly expression on his face. He stared at me a minute. Then he turned to the girl, said: "I'll be back." He picked up his hat and went out.

Judy Allen leaned down and picked up my gun from the floor. She held it by the muzzle, as if it were a croquet mallet. "How do you feel?" she asked.

"Terrible," I said.

"Are you going to tell me what happened, and why you came here?"

"No," I said. "Not now." I tried to smile at her, but my head was really pounding.

There was the buzz of her doorbell, and a pounding on the door. She walked across the room, opened the door, and two cops walked in. She waved the butt of my gun at me. "This is the man," she said.

The cops moved over to me. One of them grabbed me by the arm and pulled me to my feet. I stood still and the room swam around in big slow circles. I heard Judy Allen say: "I came home a little while ago, and there he was, on the floor. I don't know how he got in—from the fire escape, I guess. He's been shot."

One of the cops said: "Yeah, yeah. Is that his gun?"

She handed him my .38. The cop put the gun in his pocket, took out a pad and a pencil, and began to write while she gave him the story. Pretty soon he put the pad back in his pocket, said to the cop holding me by the arm: "O.K. Let's go."

They pushed me toward the door. I still felt pretty foggy, but as we went out my eyes fell on the writing desk. Something about it didn't seem right. I tried to think what it was. As they shoved me out the door, I suddenly knew. The picture of brother Jake was gone. And then I had the answer to something which had been worrying me ever since my first look at Brown Shoe. Jake Allen was not dead. Brown Shoe was Jake Allen.

CHAPTER THREE
THE WIRE SNATCHING SERGEANT

THE TWO cops took me to a hospital first. My head hurt bad, but luckily the slug had left just a short groove in my scalp above my left ear. A young interne cleaned it out, stuck some tape on it, and gave me some pills to take. Then they hauled me to the precinct hoosegow and booked me on charges of breaking and entering, carrying concealed weapons, and on general suspicion. I didn't want to tell them a thing about myself, unless they got really tough.

The boss operated a private detective agency doing special work for the government, and I was a sworn member of the U.S. Army. It never seemed very real to me, because I was doing the same kind of work I had been doing before Pearl Harbor, and I would forget for weeks on end that in Washington I was down in the books as a first lieutenant. Not that it did me any good—I couldn't even mail my letters free.

The cops worked on me a little, but I didn't tell them anything. I didn't like to phone the boss and tell him of the jam I was in. I knew he would give me hell for getting mixed up with the law—he was very touchy about that. Even in peacetime he never liked to let the cops in on a job until it was all sewed up. He always said that his methods were different, and that the police wouldn't understand them. I agreed with him on that.

They finally got tired of asking me questions and threw me into a cell by myself, I suppose because my clothes were clean and I had shaved within the last twenty-four hours. I flopped on the hard bunk and tried to figure things out. Now that I knew Jake Allen was alive the next thing I had to do was to catch him in action. I didn't get very far thinking about that, and after a while I fell asleep.

I dreamed that Captain Smythe had tied Judy Allen to a railroad track in front of an oncoming locomotive, and that I was running down the tracks after the locomotive yelling to the engineer to stop. The engineer looked out of his cab at me running down the tracks behind him and thumbed his nose at me. The engineer was Jake Allen, and in my dream I shouted: "You dirty fiend! That's your poor sister up ahead!"

I woke up in a cold sweat. The turnkey was yelling at me through the bars. "Hey! Somebody to see you."

I sat up on the bunk and looked at my wristwatch. It was one-thirty in the morning. My head felt twice as big as normal, and hurt more than ever. I yawned, ran my fingers through my hair, and looked up straight into the clear brown eyes of Judy Allen.

She was standing outside my cell door, and she still had on the same long black dress and beaver coat she had worn earlier in the evening. I said: "Hello."

She was pale, and her eyes looked tired, and a little red—as though she had been crying. She said: "Mr. Bennett, or whatever your name is, I've got to know. Why did you come to my apartment tonight?"

"Miss Allen," I said, "believe it or not, I was trying to find your brother. And I'm still sorry about your rug."

She bit her lip, and I thought she was going to start crying, but she didn't. She said: "Then you knew it, too?"

"Knew what?"

"That my brother was not dead?"

"No," I said. "But I wanted to find out."

She grabbed hold of the bars, as if she wanted to shake them. "Tell me," she said. "What's going on? What has my brother been doing? Why do you want to find him?"

I WAS thinking as fast as my banged-up head would let me, but nothing seemed to click. I was sure of only one thing—Jake Allen was not dead. I could have been mistaken about the picture, but his sister had just admitted that he was alive.

"Listen," I said, "there's plenty going on. Where was your brother about seven-forty-five tonight?"

"Why?" she asked. "Why do you want to know?"

"Because somebody took a shot at me as I was going into your place."

I thought that her face went a shade paler, and she gripped the cell bars tighter. "He was with me."

"Not at seven-forty-five, he wasn't. And what happened to Captain Smythe?"

The turnkey came up and said: "Sorry, miss. You'll have to leave now."

She said: "Mr. Bennett, if I get you out of here—now—will you tell me all you know about my brother?"

"Sure," I said. "But it isn't much." Anything, I thought, to get out of calling the boss.

She turned to the waiting turnkey. "I want to see the sergeant."

She followed the turnkey down the corridor. I straightened my necktie and waited. Three drunks who had been herded into the cell opposite me were lying on the floor and snoring loudly. The rest of the small cellblock was quiet. In a little while she came back. "I'm sorry," she said. "They won't let you out. I withdrew the breaking and entering charges, but your gun—"

"O.K.," I said. "Thanks for trying. I'll see you tomorrow."

"I can't come here tomorrow."

"I know. How about your apartment about one?"

She looked at me thoughtfully. "You seem very sure that you'll be out tomorrow."

"Sure," I said, and I grinned at her. "The mayor's my brother-in-law. I didn't want to get him out of bed tonight."

I thought I saw the ghost of a smile cross her lips, but I wasn't sure. "All right—about one."

"Will your brother be there?"

"No," she said. "You needn't be afraid. Good night, Mr. Bennett."

"Good night," I called after her.

A hoarse voice from down at the end of the row of cells cried: "Pipe down! Pipe down!"

I flopped back on the hard bunk, but I didn't sleep much. My mind was going around in circles. The first grayness of dawn was coming through the bars of the small window high over my head when I finally dozed off.

In the morning they let me out long enough to call the boss in New York. He gave me hell. But after he calmed down a little, he talked to the chief. There wasn't much trouble after that. They gave me back my gun, and I walked out into the early morning sunshine a free man.

I bought some tape, gauze and antiseptic at a drugstore, and went to my hotel. When I got my key at the desk, the clerk handed me a folded piece of hotel stationery. Across it was written in pencil: *Sorry I had to leave last night. Hope to see you again before my leave is up. Sgt. Malloy.*

I asked the clerk when the message was left.

"It was in your box this morning when I came on duty."

"What time was that?"

"Eight o'clock."

I put the note in my pocket, caught an up elevator. It was going on nine o'clock, and I was looking forward to a hot shower, a big breakfast, and maybe a couple of hours' sleep before my one o'clock date with Judy Allen.

I got out of the elevator at my floor, walked down the hall to my room, unlocked the door and went in. I was still thinking about the hot shower and the food. Suddenly I forgot all about such trivial things as breakfast.

Captain Smythe stood facing me. The morning sunlight slanting through the windows behind him glittered on the silver bars on his shoulders. He was holding a big Army .45 in his hand. Its unwavering muzzle was pointed straight at the fourth button of my vest.

CAPTAIN SMYTHE said: "Pardon the gun, Bennett. Come on in and sit down." He motioned with the gun toward a chair.

"Thanks," I said. "I'll stand. What's the play?"

"First," he said, "I want to know why you are looking for Jake Allen."

"Jake Allen?" I said. "Haven't you heard? He's dead. Killed in a plane crash at thirty-seven minutes past two."

"All right," he said, "I told you that. But we both know he's alive. What do you want with him?"

I was looking around the room. He had really gone through my stuff. Dresser drawers were standing open, my bag was open, with the contents scattered about. He had even thrown the blankets and sheets off my bed. I was glad that I never carried any identification papers—it was one of the boss' many rules.

"Find anything?" I asked. I didn't feel like answering his questions. Him and his "y" like in "eye!" I could feel the slight bulge of my .38 beneath my left arm. I began to wonder if he would shoot if I made a dive for him. I took an experimental step forward.

He stepped back and pulled the gun in close to his belly. He wasn't taking any chances. "Stand still, Bennett. For the third time—what do you want with Jake Allen?"

"Why?" I asked. I was feeling meaner by the second. I had taken enough of a beating within the last twelve hours. I began to measure the distance between us.

I could see his mouth set in a grim line, and his fingers tighten on the gun. "I'm not fooling, Bennett."

"Look, Captain," I said, "do you have to point a rod at me to ask a simple question? Put it away, and let's sit down and talk this over. I've got nothing against you—maybe we can get together."

For a minute he hesitated. I could almost see his mind working. An officer and a gentleman. The sporting thing to do, and all that. And yet I knew that he was deadly serious, that this business was very important to him. Well, it was important to me, too.

"Very well, Bennett," he said, and he tossed the gun onto the bed.

It was what I was waiting for. Maybe he felt a little foolish about pulling a gun on me in the first place, but I wasn't taking any chances. Before the gun hit the bed I stepped in and slugged him. Two swift steps took me to him, and my right found his jaw. He went down, but he wasn't out. He landed on his hands and knees, and for a few seconds he stayed that way, sort of swaying, like an old blind dog which has lived beyond its time. I picked up his gun from the bed and stood watching him, waiting for him to get up.

He didn't get up all the way. All of a sudden he lunged for me, half-crouching. It was a foolish thing for him to do. I didn't even have to lift my foot very far. I just held it up, and he ran straight into it. The heel of my shoe caught him square on the chin. He grunted and went down again, rolled over on his back. I sat down on the bed and lit a cigarette.

He lay still for a minute, his eyes open and kind of glassy. Pretty soon he got to a sitting position. There was a small cut on his chin, and I don't imagine his jaw felt any too good. He focused his eyes on me, and I waggled the gun at him.

"You play rough," he said.

"Sorry," I said. "I hate to hit a soldier, but I don't like people pointing rods at me."

He rubbed his jaw, took out a handkerchief and dabbed at his chin. He didn't attempt to get to his feet. "Very foolish of me trusting you like that," he said.

"Yeah," I said. "Very." I still felt mean. I had pulled a kind of a dirty trick on him, but in my business you have to do things like that once in a while.

The captain didn't say anything more. He just sat there dabbing at his bleeding chin. I heard a slight sound behind me. I started to turn around, but I was too late. I got a glimpse of Jake Allen leaping out of the bathroom door, which was just beyond the foot of the bed. He had a big blue steel automatic in his hand, and when I saw it he had already swung it until it was within a foot of my head.

I tried to duck but it was no use. The flat side of the gun smashed against the side of my head, and I saw a million bursting lights. My poor head, I thought. And then the room went around in whirling darkness, and for the second time in twelve hours I took the count.

WHEN I opened my eyes again, the first thing I saw was the ceiling of my hotel room. I was lying on the bed. My coat was off, and my shirt collar had been loosened. There was a damp towel around my head, and I felt terrible. I turned my head on the pillow and looked straight at Sergeant Dan Malloy.

He was sitting on a chair beside the bed, smoking a cigarette. He was staring out of the window, and he looked very trim and very neat in his uniform, with the service bar and wings pinned above his left breast pocket.

I said, "Hey, Sergeant," and he turned his head quickly and smiled. He put out his cigarette in an ashtray on a stand beside his chair.

"Hello," he said. "How do you feel?"

"Lousy. How did you get here?"

"The clerk down at the desk told me you were in, and so I came on up. Wanted to ask you to go to lunch with me. I knocked, and when you didn't answer I walked in and found you on the bed. What happened?"

I shut my eyes. My head seemed to feel better that way. "Just a little argument," I said, "with some friends."

"Some argument!" he said. "I see you carry a gun."

I opened my eyes and felt for my .38. It was still in its holster beneath my arm. "Yeah," I said. "G-Man. Want to see my badge?"

He laughed, said: "Want me to call a doctor to look at your head?"

"No, thanks. I'll be O.K. Was there anyone here when you came in?"

"No," he said.

I looked at my wristwatch. Five minutes of twelve. I had been out quite a while. I thought of my date with Judy Allen, and tried to get up. It didn't go so well. The room began to whirl around, and I flopped back on the pillow.

"Sergeant," I said, "I'm a tired old man. Will you do me a favor?"

"Sure," he said, getting to his feet.

"In my bag I think you'll find a bottle of bourbon and a box of aspirin tablets. Bring me the bottle and a couple of the tablets."

When he handed them to me I took a stiff drink of the whiskey, and two of the tablets. In a little while I felt slightly better, but not much. I took another stiff drink of the bourbon. I handed the bottle to the sergeant, got myself to a sitting position and put my feet on the floor. It was tough going, but I managed to remain that way. I took a deep breath, got to my feet, stood dizzily for a minute, and headed for the bathroom.

The cold water on my head felt swell. I yelled to the sergeant to help himself to the bourbon, and then I got my clothes off and stood under a cold shower. After that I felt fairly decent, but my head still hurt a lot.

While I was dressing, I took a couple slugs of the bourbon, and the sergeant ordered a pot of coffee and some ham and eggs. After the food and three cups of hot black coffee I began to feel almost human again.

The phone rang, and the sergeant answered it. He turned to me, said: "There's a telegram for you."

"Tell them to send it up."

In a couple of minutes the bellhop brought it in. I tossed him a quarter and ripped open the yellow envelope. It was from the Los Angeles office, and signed by George Baker. It was in code, and after I had figured it out, it read like this:

> IN FURTHER REFERENCE TO TELEPHONE CONVERSATION LAST NIGHT WISH TO ADVISE GREAT WESTERN AIRLINE CRASH RESULT OF JAMMED ALTIMETER. AIRLINE CLERK ROBERT E. WAGNER MECHANIC EARL W. SMITH UNDER ARREST. HAVE CONFESSED BEING IN PAY OF GERMAN GOVERNMENT. ALL PASSENGERS IDENTIFIED. NAME OF JAKE K. ALLEN FORGED ON PASSENGER LIST AND NOT ON PLANE.

I laid the telegram on the table beside the telephone and went on with my dressing. They had certainly gone to a lot of trouble to establish the death of Jake Allen. They had even convinced his sister that he was dead, and then had suddenly decided to let her know that he was living. I couldn't figure that out, unless they wanted to use her for something. And suddenly I didn't like the idea of Judy Allen as Nazi bait. My watch said twelve-thirty. Time for me to go.

I turned to the sergeant. He was standing by the window looking down into the street. "Sergeant," I said, "I'm sorry that I can't have lunch with you. I seem to have had mine. I'll buy you a drink later. How about the Americana about six?"

He turned from the window, picked up his cap. "Fine," he said. "See you then." He walked to the door.

I went into the bathroom to knot my tie in front of the mirror there and called out to him. "Thanks for nursing me. How about stretching that drink into dinner?"

"Swell," I heard him say. "See you at six." There was the sound of my door opening and clicking shut.

In a minute I went out into the room, picked up my hat and coat, and headed for the door. With my hand on the knob I stopped and stared at the telephone stand.

The telegram from Los Angeles was gone.

CHAPTER FOUR
DEATH JOINS THE PAYROLL

I LOOKED under the telephone directory, and in the wastepaper basket. I felt in all my pockets, and even looked in the bathroom, but I couldn't find it. I locked the door and went down the hall to the elevator.

Down at the desk I sent a short telegram to the police department of the city of Cleveland, Ohio. Then I went out to the street, snagged a taxi, and told the driver to take me to the apartment building in which Judy Allen lived. I didn't bother to ring her buzzer, but went straight up to her room and knocked. She opened the door almost immediately.

She looked swell. She was wearing pale blue pajamas under a dark blue robe. Her yellow hair was tied back of her ears with a blue ribbon. She looked about sixteen years old. When she saw me she smiled, and said: "Come in. You're right on time."

I stepped inside and she took my hat and coat, hung them in a closet, turned to me and said: "Sit down, Mr. Bennett."

I lowered my hundred and ninety pounds onto a beige-colored divan, and she sat down at the far end with one leg curled under her. In front of the divan was a low table upon which was a pair of bronze bookends holding several bright-jacketed volumes. There were also tinted glass ashtrays, a bottle of Scotch, three-quarters full, a small silver pail of ice, glasses, and a soda syphon.

She said: "Will you have a drink, Mr. Bennett?"

"Sure," I said. "But call me Jim. After all, you've known me for seventeen hours."

She laughed. "All right, Jim. Help yourself." She seemed friendly, and the strained look had gone from her eyes.

I poured Scotch into two glasses, added ice and soda, handed her one of the glasses. She said, "Thank you," and sat watching me.

I took a swallow of my drink. It was good whiskey, and I felt as though I needed it. My head was still thumping pretty badly, and I didn't feel any too good. I finished the drink in about three swallows, and made myself another. She was only sipping at hers. I set my second drink on the table, lit a cigarette, and said: "That's good whiskey, Miss Allen. You must have been hoarding it."

"No," she said. "A friend of mine left it here."

I nodded at the picture of the handsome boy on the desk. "Would his name be Jeff?"

She laughed. "You're very observing. Yes, his name is Jeff."

"What happened to the other picture?" I asked. "The one of your brother?"

The smile left her face, and in its place was the expression which I had noticed when she had visited me in the clink the night before. She took a cigarette from the box on the table, lit it, and looked at me with troubled eyes. She said: "When he saw you lying on the floor last night, he took it down and put it away."

"Why?" I wanted to know.

"I don't know," she said. "I wish I did."

"Are you worried about your brother?"

"Yes. Very much."

"Where is he now?"

"He's— I wonder why I tell you this?"

I grinned at her. "It's my open honest face and understanding nature. Go on."

"No," she said. "Really. Who are you? Why are you interested in my brother? And how did you get out of jail so easily?"

Ignoring her last question, I said: "Miss Allen, your brother is in trouble. I think you know that. It's my job to keep him from getting into more trouble."

"That's a nice way to put it," she said. "Are you going to arrest him? Are you a policeman?

I said: "A policeman wouldn't spend a night in jail—*behind* the bars."

"I don't believe you," she said, "but I seem to trust you. Are you going to arrest my brother?"

I shrugged, drained my glass, began to mix another drink. I was pretty sure that she had a good idea of the set-up, but she was being careful. "What for?" I asked.

"For whatever you think he is up to."

"Maybe," I said. "Maybe not." I was running out of answers.

Suddenly she got to her feet, walked to one of the windows, and stood looking down into the street. I sat still and watched her. She turned around and faced me. She started to talk, and she really let loose. It must have been eating at her for a long time.

"**ALL RIGHT,** Mr. Bennett," she said, "or whatever your name is. I'll tell you. I've got to tell someone, and it may as well be you. My brother is in trouble—bad trouble. I don't know what. A week ago I thought he was dead, killed in an airplane crash. I saw it in the papers, and the airline company notified me. I knew that he had been working in a war plant somewhere along the coast. The war plant blew up, or at least, a lot of it blew up, and the next thing I knew about Jake was that he was dead.

"He and I are all alone. The rest of our family is dead. Captain Smythe called me a week ago, wanted to know if I was related to Jake Allen. I told him I was his sister, and he said he wanted to talk to me about him. He met me at the club. He didn't tell me much, but he appeared to have been a friend of Jake's. I've seen a lot of the captain during this past week. He—he made love to me. He asked me more about Jake. I told him some, but not all. I didn't tell him that Jake had been in prison—for blackmail. Just before the war he became mixed up in a queer crowd. He drank a lot. I was worried about him, tried to help him. We quarreled. He went away. I didn't hear from him for over a year. My money ran out, so I went to work. Singing is the only thing I know. So I got a job singing. It's a good job, and I like it. If it weren't for Jake, I guess I would be happy."

She paused, and turned back to the window. I had taken it all in. But she hadn't told me enough. Not near enough. I said: "How did you find out that he wasn't dead?"

She answered without turning around. "Last night Captain Smythe took me home from the club. You saw us leave. He took me straight home, and then he left. I don't know where he went. I had been here a few minutes when Jake telephoned me. He wanted to know if Captain Smythe were here. He must have followed us, or had us followed. I told him that the captain had left. Then he wanted to meet me at a little bar around the corner. I met him. He told me that it was all a mistake about his being a passenger on the plane which crashed. Said he needed some money to tide him over until he got another job. I wanted to talk to him, so I brought him back here. When we came in, you were lying on the floor."

"O.K.," I said. "How about the gun you were carrying in your purse when you left the club last night?"

"Captain Smythe gave it to me four days ago. He said, rather jokingly, that a girl living by herself should have one. I kept it in my dressing room at the club. After I got the phone call from Jake I was scared. I didn't know what was going on. I thought that Jake was dead, and I knew he had been mixed up with this crowd. So I took the gun."

"You just said that you got the call here," I reminded her.

"The second one," she said, quickly. "He called me at the club first, just before I saw you by the telephone booth. I was pretty upset. I couldn't believe it was Jake, but his voice sounded like Jake's. He didn't say much, except that the plane crash story was a mistake, and that he would meet me here. He called again after I got here to make sure I was alone."

"All right," I said. "One thing more. What do you know about Captain Smythe?"

"Not too much. He told me that he had been an actor before entering the Army. Said he was now on special duty putting on entertainments at various army camps. He says he's on a thirty-day furlough, and that his home is in Trenton, New Jersey."

"Married?" I asked.

She flushed. "I don't know. He said not."

I stood up. "Thanks very much, Miss Allen. You've been very helpful. I appreciate your telling me all this, and I hope you won't be sorry. Can I ask one more question?"

She said: "Yes. Why not?"

"What do you know about Sergeant Malloy?"

"Not much. He seems all right. I've seen him around the club during the past week—always alone, until I met him with you last night."

I felt as though I ought to tell her something, after all the dope she had given me. I said: "Look, Miss Allen, I'm not a crook, and I'd like to help you. I want you to know that all this is for a good reason. I'm afraid I'll have to leave now."

She got my hat and coat and handed them to me. I held out my hand. "Good-by, and thanks again."

She took my hand, stood looking at me. I sure liked her looks. I don't have much chance to be with girls—nice girls—and Judy Allen had everything I like in a girl. I don't believe in mixing business with pleasure, and I don't know what came over me—I'm not much on the love stuff. But I pulled her towards me and I leaned down and kissed her. Her lips were soft and cool. She didn't stop me. I kissed her, and then let her go. I hadn't meant to do anything like that, but I couldn't help it.

She stood smiling at me, and I knew that my face was red. "Good-by," she said. "And stop calling me Miss Allen."

I went blindly out of the door and put on my hat and coat as I walked down the hall. Even when I got to the street, I could still feel my face burning.

When I got back to my hotel, there was an answer from my wire to Cleveland.

I TOOK the telegram up to my room. If anyone had passed me in the hall they probably would have thought I was nuts, or else playing cops and robbers. I unlocked my door, but before I went in I unlimbered my .38 and kicked the door wide open before I entered. I didn't think that I would walk into the business end of a .45 twice in the same day, but I wasn't taking any chances. Nothing happened, so I went on in. I looked in the bathroom, in the closet, and even under the bed, like any hopeful old maid, but this time I seemed to have my room to myself.

I took off my hat and coat, poured a slug of bourbon into a water glass, sat down by the desk and opened the telegram. It was signed the Cleveland Chief of Police.

> SERGEANT DANIEL MALLOY REPORTED AWOL SINCE TWENTYSIXTH. FAMILY DEAD BUT RELATIVES LIVING HERE. CHARACTER MALLOY OK. NO POLICE RECORD PREVIOUS. ARMY RECORD EXCELLENT.

I put a match to the yellow paper and watched it burn in an ashtray on the desk. Then I wrote out another telegram to the police in Trenton, New Jersey, and called a bellhop. When he came I told him to have it sent right away. I also asked him to bring me a bottle of soda water and some ice. Pretty soon he came back with the stuff, I tipped him, made myself a drink, and called the Chamber of Commerce.

They told me what I wanted to know. The nearest grinding wheel factory was The California Abrasive Products Company near a little town called Westville about forty miles northeast of San Francisco. They told me that this plant was operating under a high-priority rating and turning out valve grinding wheels by the thousands for a west-coast aircraft motor factory. I also found out that The California Abrasive Products was a branch of a big eastern outfit and had been built since Pearl Harbor in order to give quick service to the vast west-coast aircraft industry.

I called the desk to see if they could get me a car. What with gas rationing and all, they didn't know. But I carried a special "C" book, and after I told them that I had the coupons they finally rented me a 1939 Ford sedan. I told them to have it out in front in half an hour.

I shaved, took another shower, put on a clean shirt and my other suit, and went down to the lobby. At the desk I left word for Sergeant Dan Malloy, if he called, that I had been called out of town on business. When I got out in front, the car was waiting for me. It seemed to be in pretty fair shape, except that the tires looked like recapped recaps. But I figured they would hold together for forty miles, and I started out. What with the traffic and the speed laws it took me an hour and a half to get to Westville.

The California Abrasive Products had quite a layout. I counted the stacks of fourteen round kilns, and figured they must have at least one tunnel kiln. Since starting on this job I had read a lot about artificial abrasive products, and I knew what to look for. This plant was small in comparison to the big outfits, but I also knew they were specializing, and a lot of big wheels can be burned in fourteen kilns with a tunnel kiln for the big stuff. The plant covered an acre or so, and the whole works was enclosed by a high steel fence.

I pulled up to the main entranceway, parked the Ford, and walked over to the gate. A uniformed guard stopped me and asked me my business. I told him my name, and said I wanted to see the personnel manager.

"What about?" he asked.

"A job."

"All right," he said. "Wait a minute." He went inside the guardhouse and through the window I could see him telephoning. In a minute he came out and handed me a big badge with a number on it. He told me to pin it on. He gave me a printed piece of paper, said: "Have that pass signed before you leave."

I thanked him, and he let me through the gate. I walked to a door marked *Office* and went inside. A girl sitting beside a switchboard smiled at me, took my pass, talked a minute on the telephone, smiled at me again, handed me my pass, said: "Mr. Borand will see you in a few minutes."

There were a lot of chairs against the wall and I picked out one and sat down. There was also a table loaded with trade journals and advertising literature. I had time to glance through a couple of them before Mr. Borand came out. He was younger than I had thought he would be, tall, with faintly graying black hair, rimless glasses.

I stood up. "Mr. Borand," I said, "I hate to disappoint you, but I don't want a job. I want to ask a favor."

He laughed. "Maybe you've got the wrong fellow. Maybe you want to see the purchasing agent, Mr. Bayler."

"No," I said, "I'm not selling anything. Can I talk to you privately for a few minutes?"

"Sure," he said, "but we don't accept a garnishee. If a man doesn't pay his bills, we either loan him the money or fire him."

"Sorry," I said. "No bills to collect, either."

"Well, that's something," he said. "Come on."

HE LED me through a door and down a long corridor to his office. He motioned me to a chair, said: "O.K. What can I do for you?"

I told him my business, said that I didn't have any identification, but if he wanted to check he could call the San Francisco police. Before I could say any more, he broke in with: "I knew it. Another inspection. O.K., wait a minute while I call the superintendent." He sounded weary.

"No," I said, "just let me tell you. I don't want a job, I'm not collecting a bill, and I don't want to make an inspection. Right now all I want is a little information—and your promise to keep quiet about anything I might tell you."

"All right," he said, lighting a cigarette. He shoved the pack toward me. I took one, and he held the match for me.

I asked: "Did you hire any men today?"

"A few," he said. "Men are pretty scarce."

"Can you give me the names of the men you hired?"

He picked up several cards lying on his desk, said: "John Brundage, Orville Bellamy, Raymond Hudson, an old fellow named Anton Jabloski, Joseph Hausmann, and Louis Bortell. I don't know how many will show up for work. Most of them probably got a nickel an hour more someplace else and will never report. We also hired a few women."

"Never mind the women," I said. "Do you have pictures of the men?"

"I'll see," he said. He picked up a telephone, pressed a buzzer, said: "Miss Mayer, if the pictures of those new men have been sent over, bring them here, please."

We waited.

In a couple of minutes a pretty dark-haired girl came in and laid an assortment of small photographs on Borand's desk. He thanked her, handed the pictures to me, said: "These are fitted into an identification badge worn by each employee."

I picked up the pictures. The fourth one I looked at was of Jake Allen. I turned it over. On the back was written in pencil: *Louis Bortell.*

"When is this man supposed to start work?" I asked Borand.

He consulted his cards. "Louis Bortell. Tomorrow night, at seven o'clock."

"In what department?"

"Tunnel kiln."

"Do you investigate employees before hiring them?"

He shrugged. "As much as we can. If we don't hire them, someone else will. We have a lot of wheels to turn out here."

"Yes, sure," I said. "I see your position. What I want now, is this—can I come back tomorrow night and duck some place where I can watch this Bortell work without being seen?"

Borand thought a minute. "I think I can arrange it. What time you coming in?"

"About six."

He said: "I don't know what this is all about, but I guess you'll tell me when you get around to it. Anyway I'll be here tomorrow night, too."

"Fine," I said, and got up to go. "Thanks for your cooperation."

He signed my pass, handed it to me, and led me down the corridor to the reception room door. I thanked him again, went out to the gate, handed in my pass, got in the car and drove back to San Francisco.

At the hotel the clerk handed me another telegram—an answer to the one I had sent to Trenton. It said:

> CAPTAIN ANTHONY SMYTHE KNOWN HERE. SINGLE. CHARACTER EXCELLENT. ACTOR BEFORE ENTERING SERVICE. NOW ON DETACHED SERVICE ENTERTAINING TROOPS VARIOUS ARMY CAMPS. THIRTY-DAY FURLOUGH VERIFIED BY COMMANDING OFFICER.

Well, that was that. It was five-thirty. I went up to my room, washed my face, and went over to the Club Americana to keep my date with Sergeant Malloy.

CHAPTER FIVE
BOMBS AWAY

THE CLUB AMERICANA was crowded, but the white-haired waiter spotted me and got me a table close to the orchestra. Sergeant Malloy was nowhere in sight, neither was Judy Allen. I ordered a drink and sat and watched the people and looked for the sergeant. I was on my second drink when I saw him come in. He stood in the doorway and looked around the room. I raised my hand. He saw me, smiled, twisted his way between the tables and sat down beside me.

"Sorry, I'm late," he said. "Met a couple of fellows from my squadron. They just got in, but I'm due back at the base tomorrow."

"Tough luck," I said. "Why didn't you bring them along?"

"Oh, they had a couple of girls lined up. Said they might see me later in the evening."

He ordered a bottle of beer, and looked over toward the orchestra. "Isn't Miss Allen singing tonight?" he asked.

"Don't know," I said. "She hasn't so far."

He began to tell me about his two buddies. One was a radio man, and the other a turret gunner. While he was talking, the waiter came up, leaned down and spoke into my ear. "A lady wants to see you," he said in a low voice. "Out by the front door."

"Thanks," I said, and got to my feet. "Excuse me, Sergeant. Be back in a few minutes."

He smiled, said: "Sure, go ahead." I didn't know whether or not he had heard what the waiter told me.

Judy Allen was waiting for me beside the big glass doors. She was hatless, and was wearing a gray tailored suit beneath a gray tweed topcoat. There was a strained look about her eyes. It was a look which I had come to know within the last two days. I went up to her, and we didn't waste any time on preliminaries.

"What's the matter?" I asked.

"I'm sorry to bother you," she said, "but I guess you're in on this, too."

"Sure," I said. "Forget it. What's up?"

"It's the captain. He's at my apartment. He's been there all afternoon. He's—he's drunk, and acting strangely, kind of wild."

"What else?" I snapped.

"No, he hasn't bothered me. Just talks. And he won't leave."

"What does he talk about?"

"A lot of it doesn't make sense. He keeps mentioning a person named Charlie, and sometimes he'll say 'Mac,' and a lot of it is just mumbling."

"What else?"

"Nothing, except that he mentioned your name twice. He—he called you a dirty swine."

"I see," I said. "Do you want me to go back there with you?"

"Will you?"

"Sure. Just wait a minute."

I went back in to the table and told the sergeant that I had to leave. He got up, said: "I'm awfully sorry. We seem to have a hard time getting together." He held out his hand. "Well, so long. I probably won't be seeing you after tonight."

We shook hands, and I said: "The dinner is still on me. Good hunting."

I had a notion to ask him about the AWOL business, but I decided not to. On the way out I shoved a bill into the waiter's hand and told him to serve dinner to the sergeant. The checkroom girl gave me another nice smile, as she did to all the customers, but I didn't have time to make any stock cracks.

Judy Allen was still standing by the door. I took her arm, and we hit the street. The doorman snagged us a taxi, and in a few minutes we pulled up in front of her apartment building. As we went up the steps I noticed that they had put a new glass in the door which had caught the slug intended for me.

We took the elevator, and walked down the corridor to her room. When we got there we saw that the door was standing slightly ajar. She gave me a quick, puzzled look and went on in. I followed her, but first I loosened the .38 in its holster under my arm. I didn't know how tough the captain was going to get when he saw a dirty swine like me.

But I could have saved myself the worry. The captain wasn't there. The room was gray with stale smoke, and there was an empty Scotch bottle on the floor beside the sofa. Beside the bottle was a glass ashtray overflowing with cigarette stubs. Judy Allen threw her coat over a chair and walked across the room to the kitchen. I stood by the door and watched her.

She looked nice. It was the first time I had ever had a good look at her legs. They were straight and strong. I liked everything about her—the way her long, yellow hair curled over her shoulders, the tilt of her short nose, the curve of her lips. As I watched her I thought about all the years I had worked for the boss, and of all the things I'd missed. It had been just one job after another, with no time for anything but the hunt, the chase, the capture—always following the endless, sordid trail of people on the wrong side of the law.

I sighed, feeling sorry for myself, and my glance fell to the low table beside the sofa. There was a sheet of blue-tinted notepaper lying there, and on it was a message scrawled in pencil. I picked up the paper. Judy Allen's name and address were engraved across the top. The penciled words were large and shaky, and they ran all over the paper, but I made out the message: *Judy—very, very sorry… will be back later—explain—forgive me. Tony.*

JUDY ALLEN had turned from the kitchen door, and was peering into the bathroom. "Hey," I said. "You can stop looking."

She came slowly across the room and stood in front of me. I handed her the note, and she read it, a slight frown puckering her brow. Looking at her, at her bright hair and dark lashes, I forgot all about the captain, and I was thinking that maybe in a little while, when this thing was over, she wouldn't be able to stand the sight of me. But still there was something I wanted to find out. I put my hands on her shoulders. The top of her head came just below my chin. She looked up at me.

"He won't be back," I said, "but if he does, and you want me, let me know. Keep your door locked."

She smiled. "All right. Thanks for coming up with me."

"That's O.K.," I said. "Aren't you working tonight?"

"No," she said. "I'm taking the night off."

And then I asked her what I wanted to know. "Look," I said, nodding at the good-looking boy's picture on her desk, "what about that guy? Is it serious?"

"Jeff? He's in the Army now. No, it's not serious."

"Good," I said. I took a deep breath, and then I leaned down and kissed her. She didn't back away, but she didn't give me any encouragement, either. It was just a kiss—a nice, friendly kiss. "Want me to stay?" I asked.

She said, "No," gently, and stepped back. "Thanks again for coming up. Good night."

"Good night," I said, feeling like a clumsy fool. I backed up, stumbled against the door, and then I found myself in the corridor. She smiled, closed the door softly, and I heard the lock click. I went down to the elevator.

The cool night air felt swell on my burning face. I decided to walk back to the Club Americana. When I got there I saw no sign of the sergeant, so I had my dinner alone and listened to the music. After a while I paid my bill, and walked the eight or ten blocks to my hotel. In the lobby I bought a late paper and sat down in a chair behind a marble pillar. An item in the middle of page one caught my eye. It was a two column headline: NAZI AGENTS HELD IN PLANE CRASH. AIRLINE CLERK AND MECHANIC CONFESS.

The piece ran for two half-columns and enlarged on the information contained in the telegram which George Baker had sent me from Los Angeles the night before. It said that Robert E. Wagner, Great Western Airlines clerk, had admitted falsifying the passenger list record by adding the name of Jacob K. Allen in order to stop the efforts of government agents to find Allen, who was suspected of taking part in recent sabotage operations. The account said that Allen was still at large. The mechanic, Earl W. Smith, had admitted tampering with the doomed plane's altimeter which caused the pilot, Charles R. McKenner, to misjudge his height on the mountainous Albuquerque run and crash into a hilltop eight miles north of that city killing himself, the co-pilot, and twelve passengers.

Another item in the paper attracted my attention, but it didn't mean anything to me at the time. It was a small piece on page three.

BODY STILL UNIDENTIFIED

The body of a man, about 30, which was found by police in an alley in the dock district three days ago, is still lying unidentified in the county morgue. When found, the body was completely naked. Death was due to a blow on the head.

I stuck the paper in my pocket, went up to my room, got into pajamas, and wrote a letter to the boss in New York. I told him all that happened up until now, and what I intended doing. When I was on a job I always did this, because I never knew what would turn up, or how things were going to turn out for me, and I wanted the boss to know in case anything went wrong. I gave him all the dope—what had happened, what I thought. When I had finished, I stuck an air mail stamp on it, went out in the corridor, dropped the letter down the mail chute, and went to bed.

I SLEPT late the next morning, had a combination breakfast and lunch, read all the papers, slept some more. I got dressed about four in the afternoon, called the desk and told them to bring the Ford around, went down to the street, climbed behind the wheel and started for Westville.

I thought some about calling Judy Allen, but decided not to.

I pulled up at the main gate of The California Abrasive Products Company around a quarter of six. There was a different guard on duty, and I had to go through the whole routine again. But Borand was waiting for me. The office didn't work at night, just the plant, and he took me back through the dark corridor to his office.

Borand said: "I don't mind telling you that I checked with the San Francisco police, and I want to help you in any way I can."

I said, "Thanks," and he put out a bottle of whiskey and some glasses. We had a couple of drinks. He called the main gate and told the guard on duty to call him the minute that Louis Bortell reported for work, and then we talked about different things, this and that.

He seemed O.K., just one of the many unsung men charged with the responsibility of keeping the war plants running—men who work long hours getting the stuff needed to produce the tools of war moving out to the industrial fronts. He said he had intended to work tonight anyhow, and had had a bottle of milk and a sandwich sent in for his dinner.

After a while his telephone rang. It was the guard at the main gate, and I could hear his voice. "Mr. Borand? Louis Bortell just checked in."

Borand said, "Thanks," hung up, and looked at me. "O.K. He's here. I'll take you down and show you the hiding place we've fixed up for you. Do you think he'll try anything tonight?"

I said. "I've got a hunch that tonight's the night. It's getting a little hot for him. The papers broke the story today. He'll probably try to do the job tonight, and get the hell out."

Borand nodded. "I'll take you down."

I followed him out of the office and down a long flight of steps to the plant floor. He opened a big sliding door and we were in a maze of roaring confusion.

"Finishing room," Borand shouted at me.

I saw an acre of machines, with a man or a woman at each machine. They were cutting the rough grinding wheels down to exact size. Borand led me through an aisle between the finishing lathes, and we entered a quieter section of the factory. Here men and women were inspecting the finished wheels for flaws. We walked past the huge testing drums where the wheels are put on spindles and revolved at twice the commercial operating speed to see that they won't break in operation. "When they break," Borand said, "it's like bullets flying. Those metal drums protect the operators doing the speed testing. If they don't break at that speed, they're O.K. to ship."

I nodded, and kept following him. We came out into a vast room filled with big kilns. Some of them showed red fire between the cracks of the fire doors. It was very hot.

"Round kilns," Borand said. "Tunnel kilns over there."

We walked along a cement ramp between the kilns until we came to an open space. Here two white-tiled structures ran back into the darkness, with massive air pipes leading into them at intervals. There were steel tracks along the sides of the kilns and on the tracks were small cars loaded with grinding wheels waiting their turn to be burned.

Borand said: "Those cars carry the green wheels through the kilns at the rate of three feet a minute. When they come out at the other end they are ready to be sent to the finishing room. All of the wheels on the cars on this whole track are to be used in the finishing of aircraft motors."

I looked at my watch. It was a quarter of seven. At the mouth of the kiln two men were busy transferring green soft wheels from tiered wooden racks to the tunnel kiln cars. They removed the small valve grinding wheels from the racks and placed them very carefully in sand-filled containers on the kiln cars.

"How hot does it get inside those kilns?" I asked Borand.

"About twenty-four hundred degrees, Fahrenheit," he said. "Here's where you hide."

He led me to a big round kiln. It was empty, and no fires were burning beneath it. He walked up three stone steps and stooped to enter a small opening. I followed him. The inside of the kiln was circular, and the floor was paved with bricks. Borand pointed out a small hole bored into the brick wall. I looked through the hole and I had a perfect view of the mouth of the tunnel kiln.

Borand said: "That's where Bortell will be working. This kiln won't be fired for a couple of days. Nobody will bother you."

"O.K.," I said. "How long are you going to be around?"

"All night," he said. "If anybody is going to try to blow up a tunnel kiln, I want to be around."

"Fine," I said, "but nobody's going to blow it up while I'm here. All I want to do is to catch him in the act of *trying* to blow it up."

Borand said: "If you want me, there's a phone at the end of this ramp."

"O.K," I said, "and thanks."

"Look," he said, "shall I send in a couple of guards? Maybe you'll need some help."

"No, thanks," I said. "If I need any help, I'll call you."

"All right," he said. "See you later."

He went away and I settled down to waiting and watching. At seven o'clock a whistle blew, and I saw a man, evidently a foreman, come up with two men and talk to one of the men already working. Apparently the foreman was introducing the two new men to the old worker. In a little while the foreman went away, and I saw the old worker point to the tunnel kiln cars. One of the new men nodded understandingly. I was about fifty feet away, but I recognized this man instantly.

It was Jake Allen.

FROM MY peep hole inside the kiln I watched the three men working. Beside Jake Allen there was an old man with white hair and a white mustache. He didn't seem to know much about the job, and the man who had stayed to instruct the two men was talking to him and demonstrating the proper method of placing the wheels in the sand-filled containers on the tunnel kiln cars. Jake Allen went right ahead with the work as if he knew all about it, as he probably did. After a while the instructor went away and left Allen and the old man by themselves.

The two men loaded six cars and pushed them into the kiln, and started to load the seventh. They worked a little while together, with Allen talking and pointing for the white-haired man's benefit, apparently showing him the fine points of placing grinding wheels on tunnel kiln cars.

I watched and waited. It was dark in the kiln, and hot. By the light coming through the hole in the kiln's wall, I looked at my watch. Ten minutes past eight. I looked out of the hole again, and I saw what I had been waiting for.

Allen was pointing across the big kiln building to the far side, apparently telling the old man to go over and perform some duty or other, maybe to get something. Anyway, it appeared to me as though Allen were getting his aged helper out of the way, at least for the time being. I loosened my .38 in its holster and glued my eye to the hole.

The old man began walking away. He was stooped, and he walked with a slow, shuffling gate. When he was about twenty feet away, Allen walked swiftly to his coat, which was lying in a bundle beside some wooden wheel racks. From the coat he took a small square box, hurried back to the car which they had just loaded and which was standing on the track at the mouth of the tunnel kiln. I could hear the roaring of the gas jets inside the kiln, and I saw the white heat showing through the air vents. As I watched, Allen placed the small box beneath the steel bottom of the car. He took some wire from his pocket and began to wire the box in place. That was what I was waiting for. I was on the point of leaving my hiding place, when something happened which caused me to watch a little longer.

The old man who had been walking away from Allen suddenly wheeled around and came running back. I remember being surprised that an old guy could move so quickly. In a second he was upon Allen, and I saw his fist come around and strike Allen in the face. Allen stumbled back against the kiln car and began jerking at something beneath the front of his overalls. The old man bored in, struck Allen again. I waited no longer.

I ran out of the kiln doorway, down the few steps to the cement ramp, and headed for the two men. Even as I ran, I saw the gleam of metal in Allen's hand. There was a sharp hollow report which reverberated against the walls of the vast kiln room, and I saw the orange stab of flame. But the old man bored right on in. I saw him chop at Allen with both fists, and Allen went down.

I shouted, "Hey!" and for the first time the old man saw me running toward him. He turned, and very deliberately drew a gun from his overalls pocket, leveled it, and fired. A faint sigh breathed past my ear.

I had my .38 in my hand then, and I kept on coming. Out of the corners of my eyes I could see men running from all corners of the plant. The old man fired again, and I dropped to my hands and knees. Up on the cement ramp I made a perfect target. Then I heard a voice, a strangely familiar voice, "Bennett," the old man called. "Stay where you are, or I'll kill you."

I rolled off the ramp and landed on my feet running. A five-foot cement wall now protected me, and I ran, stooping, until I reached the platform beneath the tunnel kiln tracks. I climbed up, my gun in my hand.

At that moment I saw Allen get to his hands and knees, saw him raise his hand, and heard the hammering roar of his gun. The old man swayed on his feet, but he didn't go down. His gun spat flame, and Allen slid slowly forward on his face. In almost the same instant the old man turned his gun on me, and chips of cement struck me in the face. I steadied my .38, squeezed the trigger, and the white-haired man collapsed.

A crowd of workers rushed up as I climbed up on the cement runway. They gathered around, and as I pushed through them I caught sight of Borand. He made a path for me. While they lifted Jake Allen from the floor, I looked closely at the old man lying by the kiln car. His overalls were bloody, high up on his chest, where my slug had caught him, and there was another wound on his hip. The man looked faintly familiar to me, but I didn't have time to think about it. I leaned down and felt beneath the kiln car. I found the box, and men helped me unwire it.

"Time bomb," I said to Borand. "Get some water."

A man came running with a bucket of water, and I placed the box very gently in it. Borand gave some orders, and the workers cleared out and went back to their machines. A uniformed guard came up.

I motioned to the forms of Allen and the old man. "They look harmless now, but you'd better watch them."

He nodded, and pulled out a businesslike looking rod. To Borand I said: "Better get the plant doctor, if you have one."

"He's on the way. Anything else?"

"Yeah. Call the police. I'll be back." I started away.

"Need any help?" asked Borand.

"Don't know yet. Maybe. I'll holler."

I went through the plant and out to a side gate. I showed my pass to the guard on duty. "What's going on in there?" he asked.

"Not much," I said. "Listen, if you hear any shooting out on the road, come a-running."

Out on the highway I began to move slowly around the plant. It was very dark. I walked on the grass along the edge of the road trying to see ahead of me into the darkness. I had covered two sides of the plant and I could see the lights of the main gate guardhouse up ahead of me. And then I smelled the odor of burnt gasoline, and I stopped for a moment and listened.

From up ahead came the faint sound of a motor running. I walked forward very slowly, my .38 in my hand. Presently I saw the outline of a car at the edge of the road ahead. It was parked well off the road, almost in the shallow ditch, with no lights on, and the sound of the running motor came louder to me. I walked up slowly behind it.

I couldn't tell if anyone was sitting in the car. There was enough light from the main gate of the plant to tell me that no one was behind the wheel. The car was a sedan, and I looked in the rear window. The rumble of the many machines in the plant came very faintly out to me. The sound blended with the soft purr of the car's motor. There was no other sound.

I felt a sudden, hard pressure in the middle of my back. A voice said: "Stand still."

CHAPTER SIX
GI DOUBLECROSS

I DIDN'T stand still. I was in this business deep, and I couldn't take any chances. Whoever was waiting out here to take Jake Allen away as soon as he had planted his time bomb in the tunnel kiln was in it deep, too. Too deep to monkey much with a snooping dick like me. I figured I was lucky not to have been shot in the back while I stood looking into the car, and I figured, also, that that was the end of my luck.

A split second after the gun had prodded my backbone I dropped to my knees, turning as I dropped. And as I turned I charged forward, as I used to do when I played left tackle back east ten years before. The guy behind me with the gun went over backwards, and his gun cracked loudly in the silent night. A bright flash burned past my eyes, and then I was on him. I brought my .38 around in a wide arc and slammed it against his head. But he was twisting and squirming under me, and I felt my gun glance off. With my left hand I was trying to grab his gun arm and pin it down, but I couldn't locate it, and both of us squirmed and grunted and fought savagely and silently.

I was still trying to grab his gun arm when there was a muffled explosion. The whole left side of my body suddenly seemed to be on fire. He must have had the muzzle of his rod right in my vest pocket. I could smell the sudden odor of burnt cloth. I found his wrist then, and I pushed backwards and upwards. I kept pushing his arm back and across until I heard a distinct snapping sound. He cried out, and I let loose of the arm then, and slammed my .38 down against the outline of his head. I hit him square this time, and smacked him again for good measure. He lay very still beneath me.

Suddenly I didn't feel so good. I could feel the inside of my vest getting wet, and there was a dull pain all along my side. I fumbled for the wound. It was at the outer edge of my belt line, above my hip. I brought my fingers away, and they were wet. I fished out a handkerchief, held it against my side, and got slowly to my feet.

I could hear men running down the road, and I saw the flare of an electric torch. Two of the plant guards came running up and flashed the light on us. I said, "Here's another one, boys," and felt myself swaying on my feet.

They turned the guy over, and for the first time I saw that he was dressed in the uniform of the United States Army. The light hit his bloody face. It was Sergeant Dan Malloy.

I heard the wail of a siren and saw a police car wheel into the drive and stop at the main guardhouse. I walked down the road to the gate. The road seemed to be heaving up and down under my feet, but I made it to the entranceway. The guard was opening the gate for the cops.

"Hey!" I yelled.

One of the cops got out of the car and walked toward me. I heaved my arm. "Over in the ditch. Guy in an Army uniform."

"Who are you?" asked the cop.

"Never mind," I said, wearily. "Get that guy. I'll go into the plant with your buddy."

He was a young cop. He looked doubtful. "All right," I said. "You can check with Borand. But I think that guy in the ditch will need a little medical attention."

"How about you?" he asked.

"Me, too," I said, and climbed into the car beside the other cop. "Straight ahead," I said to him.

He didn't ask any questions. We pulled up by the kiln entrance. "Tell Borand I want to see him," I told the cop. The car seat felt nice and soft, and I was afraid that if I got out of the car I would never make it back in again. The cop went in the plant, and I just sat and waited. I could feel the blood soaking through my handkerchief and running over my fingers.

Borand came out in a minute. He looked in the window at me. "Hey," he said, "you're hurt."

"Yeah," I said. "That doctor still in there?"

"He's got both of those fellows over in the first aid room. I think one of them is dead."

"Which one?" I asked. My voice sounded as though it were coming from far out in the darkness of the night.

"The young one," I heard Borand say. "The one called Bortell."

Borand went away then, and in a minute he came back. "Doc will be right out."

"Thanks," I said. "How's the other one doing?"

"Doc says he thinks he'll be all right."

"Good," I said. "That's good."

I heard Borand say, "What?" and it seemed to me that I was floating away, high in the dark sky, and Judy Allen was somewhere ahead of me, floating, too. I heard her laugh. I started to laugh, too, and then I stopped laughing because a red curtain of pain dropped before my eyes, and Judy

Allen was gone, and the night was gone, and then there was nothing.

I OPENED my eyes to blinding white light. I blinked, and I heard a voice say: "He's conscious now, Doctor."

I turned my head. I was lying on a narrow bed in a small room and everything around me was white—walls, ceiling, the dazzling light hanging directly over me. A girl in a white dress and cap was standing beside my bed. She was short and wide and not pretty, but she had a nice smile. At the foot of the bed stood Borand and beside him was a young man I hadn't seen before. The young man had on a white jacket, and he was smoking a cigarette. He wore thick-lensed glasses, and was almost bald.

Borand said: "Well, Bennett."

I started to raise myself up, but the young man with the glasses stepped quickly forward and gently held me down. "You can't do that," he said. "Not for a while. You've lost a lot of blood."

I could hear a faint humming noise from beyond the room. Sometimes it was low and deep, and then it would rise to a shrill metallic scream. "Where am I?" I said, just like in the movies, but I really wanted to know.

"At the plant," said Borand, "First aid room."

"That noise," I said. "Finishing room?"

Borand grinned, said: "Yep. You're learning fast."

Things were beginning to come back to me, and suddenly I wanted to know a lot of things. "Hey—" I began.

Borand said: "Not now. You're going to the hospital."

The nurse leaned down with a glass of water, and a big white pill. "Here," she said, "take this."

I took it obediently, and closed my eyes. I didn't go to sleep, and I didn't pass out, but I just didn't feel like bothering much about anything. I know they carried me out, and I had the sensation of movement, and after a while there was another white room and another white-clad nurse.

I was in a long room, and there was a lot of talking going on. I looked up at the ceiling, and felt as though I just wanted to lie there in that nice soft bed for the rest of my life. Borand came up beside me and stood looking down. "How do you feel?" he asked.

"O.K. Kinda tired." I turned my head and looked around the room. There were six beds besides my own, and two of them were occupied. A nurse and the bald-headed doctor were fussing around the bed next to mine. Borand saw me looking. He said: "Your pals."

"Yeah?"

"Sure. Jabloski, and the guy you ran into out by the fence."

"Oh," I said. I was beginning to feel better, but I still didn't feel like doing a lot of talking. The doctor came up and leaned over me.

"How you doing?" he asked.

"All right. My side hurts some."

"It's nasty," he said. "Better have another tetanus shot." His voice faded away.

The nurse stepped up, and the doctor worked quickly and expertly. I closed my eyes.

When I opened them the doctor and the nurse were gone, but Borand was still standing there. Beside him stood a big, red-faced man, chewing on a cigar. Borand said: "Chief Dawson, Westville Police."

I said: "Hi, Chief."

The red-faced man nodded sourly, chewed on his cigar, said: "Heard of you, Bennett. Met your boss once."

I heard a peculiar sound beside me. It was a rasping, strangling sound, and I turned my head. My eyes were focusing a little better, and I saw that Sergeant Malloy was lying in the bed next to mine. His head was bandaged, and there was a sheet pulled up to his chin. He was staring straight at the white-painted ceiling with bright, feverish eyes. His mouth was open, and the sound of his heavy breathing filled the room. I couldn't see much of the person in the next bed.

Borand moved around to my side, leaned down, and said in a low voice: "Next to him is Jabloski, the old guy. Only he isn't old at all. A young fellow, with a false mustache, powdered hair and stage makeup—did you know that?"

"No," I said, "but I wondered. How about Allen, the guy you called Bortell?"

"Dead," said Borand. "Jabloski's bullet got him smack in the heart. It's a queer setup. I hired Bortell for kiln work, and right after that Jabloski came in and asked for kiln work, so I hired him, too. After the shooting last night we carried both of them to the first aid room, but Bortell—or Allen, as you call him—was already dead. Jabloski was hit twice—in the hip by Allen, and the chest by you, but not bad. Doc thinks he'll be all right. This fellow next to you, the one you had the fight with outside, is not doing so good. He made a break, and the cops shot him. You feel like hearing more?"

I nodded my head.

"Well, this Bortell, or Allen, was pretty smart. He knew that the heat of the kiln would explode his time bomb before it reached the center of the kiln, and so he wired it beneath the steel bottom of the car, so that the heat wouldn't affect it. This is the damnedest thing that ever happened in a plant where I worked, but I suppose it could happen any place."

"Yeah," I said. "It could. And does. Where are we, in the hospital?"

"Yes," said Borand. "In Westville. Accident ward."

"What about him—Malloy?" I motioned with my head toward the bed next to me.

"We don't know yet. He apparently was waiting outside to help Bortell, or Allen, make a getaway."

The doctor stepped up. He spoke in a low voice to Borand and the Chief. "You'll have to hurry. He can talk now, but I won't guarantee for how long."

The Chief nodded, clamped his teeth down on his cigar, and moved over beside Malloy's bed. Borand followed him. The doctor stood by. The room was suddenly very quiet. The only sound was Malloy's heavy, irregular breathing. He'd take a couple of deep, gasping breaths, then a short one, and for a couple of seconds you'd think he had stopped. Then there would be a deep, strangling inhalation, and it would start all over again. It wasn't nice to listen to.

A YOUNG cop wearing glasses stepped up to the other side of Malloy's bed. He had a notebook and a pencil in his hand. He held the pencil poised, and there was a bright, expectant look on his chubby face. The Chief bent over Malloy and said: "Can you hear me?"

I saw Malloy nod slightly, his feverish stare on the ceiling.

"What is your name?"

"Ludwig Gebhart." The words were surprisingly clear in the stillness of the room. The young cop wrote in his book.

"All right." The Chief's voice was not unkind. "Ludwig, you know that you haven't long to live?"

Malloy, alias Gebhart, nodded again, still staring at the ceiling. He gulped convulsively, and the words came out strong and clear. "Heil, Hitler!"

There was silence in the room. The doctor, the young cop, a nurse in the background, the Chief, Borand and myself were all watching the man on the bed. I heard the Chief mumble to Borand: "I'll be damned! A regular Natsy."

Suddenly Gebhart began to talk. The words came in a rush, broken by his labored breathing. Some of it I couldn't get, but I got enough. The young cop scribbled furiously, and the rest listened intently. He began: "I die for the glory of the Third Reich. But I do not die in vain. Others will carry on my work..."

I heard it all, and I read the typed transcript afterwards. Sometimes he stopped completely while he labored for breath, sometimes his voice was so low that it was only a whisper in the silent room. But he kept on, spasmodically, painfully, gasping for breath, until the story was told, with his bright eyes always on the ceiling. Occasionally, a grim smile would twist his lips, and once he laughed, a short, bitter laugh, but he told it all. This was his story:

He was German-born, but naturalized, had gone to American schools. He had been working with a crowd of Nazi agents with headquarters in San Francisco. His group had contacted Jake Allen, put him on their payroll. Allen pulled a couple of jobs for them, and then things got hot. They knew that we had our eyes on Allen—that's when I went on the job. Allen was a good man, clever with kilns especially, and so they attempted to establish his death in order to put us off his trail. The two Nazis working for the aircraft company took care of that. It didn't matter to them that they killed fourteen people doing it. They knew that

Allen had a sister, but they didn't trust her. That's where Gebhart came in.

They killed the real Sergeant Malloy in an alley off the docks, stripped him, took his papers and uniform, and Gebhart turned into Malloy. It was his job to keep an eye on Judy Allen, and at the same time be around to help Jake Allen pull the California Abrasives job. The uniform was good cover. He drove the getaway car, and he and Allen had planned to pull out as soon as the bomb was planted. I put the jinx on that.

Near the end Gebhart said: "We knew about Bennett, and whom he worked for. I am sorry that I missed him when I shot at him outside my comrade's sister's apartment—and in her apartment, too. That was my first mistake. I should have killed him then, but I failed. I should have killed him in his hotel room, when I had the chance. But it was not a good place to do it, and the time for our work was too near. I couldn't take the chance then." His voice had dropped to a hoarse whisper, and the words came slower and slower, then died out. There was a moment's silence in the room. Then Gebhart coughed, and the doctor stepped forward. We heard Gebhart say: "I have failed, but I die happy. I die for Der Fuehrer."

The doctor felt Gebhart's pulse and then turned and looked at us. He nodded slowly, his lips tight. Gebhart's eyes were still open, but we could no longer hear his breathing. There was a smile on his young face. The doctor drew up the sheet and nodded to the nurse. She came over and wheeled the bed out of the room. The young chubby-faced cop stuck his notebook in his hip pocket and helped her.

The Chief chewed on his cigar. "Damnedest story I ever heard. They take a lot of killing. Bennett, you're lucky." He jerked a thumb at the occupant of the other bed. "What about that guy? Jabloski, is it? The false face artist. Where does he fit in?"

I looked across at Jabloski's bed. He turned his face toward me for the first time. Only it wasn't Jabloski any longer. The white mustache was gone, and his hair was black. It was Captain Anthony Smythe, and he looked very pale against his pillow.

He grinned at me. "How's the G-Man?"

I said: "Captain, you did a good job on Allen, but you're a rotten shot. That second slug of yours missed me a foot."

"Sorry I can't say the same about you," he said. "I guess I had you figured all wrong."

"How?"

"When I first met you at the club the other night I thought you were in with Allen."

"You were pretty friendly with Allen, too."

"Yes, but I had a reason. I knew he was mixed up in the plane crash, and I was watching him. I made friends with him so that I could watch him better. I made a play for his sister, too, and Allen and I got real friendly. I didn't know what your business was, and I didn't trust you. You see, I was working alone. I knew that Allen didn't completely trust you, either. I thought that was the reason he helped me in your hotel room. Before that I thought you were working with Allen. After he smacked you, I didn't know what to think."

"Neither did I," I said. "How did you know that Allen wasn't in the plane crash?"

"A close friend of mine who works for Great Western tipped me off before the papers got it. He also told me that Allen had a sister, and so I thought that by hanging around her I could get a line on her brother. I was right. Allen showed up. The people who were paying him shut off his money until he finished this last job. He was broke, and so he contacted his sister."

"Did you give her a gun?" I asked.

"Yes. When I heard that Allen was alive I didn't know what she might get into. She was a nice girl, and I liked her. I gave her the gun because if she got into trouble it would be partly my fault. She knew nothing of the racket her brother was in. I knew that Allen was going to get a job at California Abrasives, and so I followed him out here and got a job, too. I wanted to know for sure that he was mixed up in this thing, I wanted to get him in the act. He was the reason for the plane crash, and the only one of the bunch I could get at. I used to be on the stage, so I put on some makeup when I applied for the job. When I saw him planting that bomb I lit into him."

HE STOPPED talking. He look tired. The Chief said: "This is all very chummy, but I gotta get back to the station. Bennett, is he in the clear?"

"What do you think?" I asked. "He got Allen, didn't he?"

"O.K.," said the Chief. "I'll see you tomorrow." He and the young cop went out.

Borand left, too, saying that he would see me later. Only the doctor and the nurse remained. The doctor said: "You fellows better get some sleep. We'll take you upstairs—there's a room ready for you."

"All right," I said. "In a couple of minutes." I turned toward the captain. His eyes were closed. "Look, Captain. Maybe I'm talking out of turn, but why did you— What about yesterday afternoon?"

He opened his eyes. "I'm sorry about that. I was so mixed up, and I wanted to wind this thing up so badly, that I guess I sort of snapped. I got drunk—good and drunk, and I went to Judy Allen's apartment. It was a hell of a thing to do, but I guess I thought maybe she could help me. I don't remember much after that. I hope I wasn't too bad."

"No," I said. "You weren't too bad. How do you feel now?"

"Pretty good. My leg hurts the worst—high up, close to my hip. That's where Allen got me."

"One thing more," I said. "Why did you want to mess in this in the first place?"

He turned and looked at me. "I had a good reason. My best friend was pilot of that plane. Grew up with him, went to school with him. He married my sister. They have a two-year-old son—I mean, she has, now. His name is Tony."

I thought of what Judy Allen had told me about the names he had repeated at her apartment. "Would his name be Charlie, or Mac?"

"Yes. Charles McKenner. Did you see it in the papers?"

"Yes," I said.

He closed his eyes, and I said to the doctor: "How about that room?"

The next morning they brought me the papers. The story was all over the front pages. They had pictures of everybody, including Judy Allen. The story was all messed up, but it didn't make any difference to me. It was over, and I was glad of it. I had a nurse send a telegram to the boss, and I wondered what he would cook up for me next.

Along about noon the nurse said I had a visitor. Sure enough, it was Judy Allen. She was dressed in black, and she was pale. Her red lips stood out darkly against her white face. But she was still the best-looking girl I had ever seen.

I said, "Hello," and she came over and stood by my bed.

"How are you?" she asked.

"O.K," I said.

There was a silence. I didn't know what to say. After a bit I said: "I'm sorry."

She sat down in the chair beside my bed and folded her hands in her lap. "Don't be," she said. "I don't blame you."

"Thanks."

"Don't talk about it," she said softly.

"Captain Smythe's here," I said.

"Yes, I know."

"Have you seen him?"

"No."

There was an awkward silence. "Look," I said, "I'll be out of here in a couple of days. Can I see you?"

"Yes," she said, and she smiled.

I smiled, too. Suddenly everything was all right again. I felt happy.

"Aren't you going back to New York?" she asked.

I shrugged. "I don't know. I think I'll ask the boss if I can't be transferred to Italy, or France, or some place. I need a rest."

She laughed, and I looked at her and thought about how pretty she was.

MURDER WITHOUT MUSIC

SHARP-EYED PRIVATE DETECTIVE BENNETT TRAVELS FAST TO CATCH UP WITH A RUTHLESS GANG OF PRECISION TOOL THIEVES—AND IS PLUNGED INTO A GRIM HAIRSBREADTH STRUGGLE FOR SURVIVAL!

CHAPTER ONE
FAT MAN'S MONEY

THE RINGING of the telephone awakened me. I switched on the light at the head of my bed and looked at my wrist-watch. Seven minutes of three—in the morning. I turned off the light, rolled over, and tried to go back to sleep again. But the telephone kept on ringing. I sighed, crawled out of bed, and pressed the wall button which switched on the overhead light of the hotel room. I crossed the room and picked up the receiver.

"Yeah."

"Jim?" said a voice. "This is Art."

"For the love of Mike," I said. "Go back to bed."

"Jim, listen. Can you come over right away?"

"Oh sure," I said. "Look, Art, I just got in from the Coast. I've been in bed one hour. I'll see you tomorrow."

"Jim, I've got trouble."

"What kind of trouble?"

"Bad trouble, Jim. I wish you'd come over."

Art Haynes was a good friend of long standing, and he sounded worried. I cast a longing look at my bed.

"Okay," I said. "You at the terminal?"

"Yes."

"Be there in ten minutes."

I piled into the clothes which I had taken off an hour before, slipped my old .38 into an inside coat pocket, took an elevator down to the lobby, tossed my key at the sleepy desk clerk, and hit the sidewalk. Five minutes later I got out of a cab in front of the Cleveland terminal of the Haynes Truck Lines.

Art was standing on the curb waiting for me. He was a man in his middle thirties, about my own age, a little under six feet, with wide powerful shoulders. His thick black hair was beginning to gray a little at the temples.

He shook hands with me.

"Thanks for coming Jim," he said. "How're things on the Coast?"

"Where's the body?" I asked.

Art climbed behind the wheel of a blue convertible parked at the curb.

"You dicks are all alike," he said. "Come on."

I got in beside him. Art didn't say anything and I didn't ask any questions. I was still sleepy. We drove about eight blocks and turned into the driveway. The headlights hit a big brick house with lots of lawn in front.

I saw a black-and-gold sign sticking in the grass, and the gold lettering glittered briefly, DE LANCEY FUNERAL HOME. The place was dark except for a light in the rear. We drove around to the back, parked the car on a cement ramp, and Art got out and rang a bell.

In a couple of minutes a short pudgy, pink-faced man opened the door. He was wearing rubber gloves and a white apron. The apron was stained and greasy-looking. When he spoke his voice sounded greasy, too.

"Yes, gentlemen," he inquired.

I cut loose with the .38 in my coat pocket.

Art introduced himself and nodded at me. "This is Jim Bennett, a private detective, and a good friend of mine. We'd like to see Westover's body."

De Lancey rubbed his gloved hands together. Even at three-thirty in the morning he acted like an undertaker.

"Yes, yes, gentlemen. I'm preparing the body now. Very regrettable indeed. Come this way, please."

We followed him inside and down a short flight of steps and entered a long, white-painted basement room. The room was lined with glass-enclosed shelves of bottles, jugs and various equipment. On a long, white, enameled table lay the body of a young man. I figured him to be about twenty-seven.

He was powerfully built, and even in death his body gave the impression of muscular hardness. There was a curious flatness to the top of his skull. There was no blood—the undertaker had taken care of that—but it was easy to see what had caused his death.

"Looks like they used a ball bat," I said to Art.

"He was a good boy," Art said. "One of my best drivers. Been with me for eight years. Nice wife, two swell kids—it's a crying shame."

"Tough," I said. "What happened?"

"We don't know—the police don't know."

"If the cops are on it, why drag me in?"

ART SMILED at me. He looked tired, and there was a black stubble on his usually smooth-shaven face.

"The police haven't found out a thing. It's been going on for a month. This is the climax." He nodded at the body on the table. "I knew you were out on the Coast, but your office told me you'd be back tonight. I wanted to see the body before the—before Mr. De Lancey fixed it up—prepared it. I told the police I was calling you in, and I want it to be a regular job. Name your fee."

"The Boss accepts the jobs," I said. "And he names the fees. But he's out of town. I'll do what I can. But I've got to have the whole story."

"Come on," Art said.

He thanked De Lancey, and we started for the door. The undertaker bowed us out. We climbed into the car, drove back to the terminal, and went into Art's office. He took a bottle of bourbon from his desk, poured out two slugs.

"Thanks," I said and downed my drink. He poured another.

"This is the story," he said. "We've been shipping a lot of high priority stuff to Detroit: diamond tool bits, precision tools, micrometers—stuff like that. Mostly tool bits. All of it comparatively scarce and all of it worth lots of dough. We pick it up in Pennsylvania and New York State, bring it this far, load it on a freight car which takes it directly into Detroit.

"I've got a deal with the railroad and it gives the boys in Detroit a little faster service. At the same time it makes room on my trucks for other important freight. It worked swell for quite a while.

"Then about a month ago we began to lose stuff—whole shipments, sometimes part shipments, of tool bits and precision tools. The car with our stuff is sealed here, and when it arrives in Detroit the seals are unbroken. Yet the stuff is gone when the car is opened."

"All small stuff—easy to carry away?" I asked.

"Yes, but it doesn't take a very big stack of tool bits, for example, to amount to plenty of money. It's about driving me nuts. The cops can't find out a thing. Neither can the railroad dicks. The insurance boys are raising the devil—talking of canceling my contracts. If they do, I may as well quit business."

"Have you tried sending a man along with the car?"

"Yes, we tried that—twice. The first time a couple of the railroad detectives rode in the car to Detroit. Nothing happened. Our stuff arrived okay. And then a couple of days later we lost another batch of diamond tool bits."

"What happened the second time?"

"I just showed you what happened. That boy was murdered. Orville—that's his first name—wanted to try his luck. He wanted to go along with the car. We said okay. Yesterday afternoon he got in the car with our shipment, and we sealed him in. When the car arrived in Detroit our stuff, or most of it, was gone. And my boy was dead. Both doors of the car were sealed up tight."

"Was Westover armed?"

"Yes. We gave him a gun, but it wasn't fired."

"It could have been an accident."

"That's what the cops claimed. They thought he might have fallen against something, maybe when the train made a curve. I don't think so. Do you?"

"I don't know," I said. "Does that freight make any stops between here and Detroit?"

"No. Fast freight. Straight through."

"What are you going to do now?"

Art shrugged.

"That's why I called you. I've got to do something, but fast. Westover's brother, Pete, wants to go along with the next shipment."

"Does he work for you too?"

"Yes."

"Are you going to let him go?"

"I don't know. What do you think?"

"When's the next shipment going out?"

"Tomorrow— I mean today. Three o'clock in the afternoon."

"It's up to you whether he goes or not. If he goes, tell him to watch himself. I'll see you tomorrow. I want to be on hand when you load that car. And you better go home and get some sleep."

"All right," he agreed. "There's nothing I can do here tonight."

We went outside, got in the car, and headed uptown. Art left me at my hotel, and I went on in and up to my room. I unlocked the door, switched on the lights, took off my hat and coat. I had my shirt unbuttoned when somebody knocked on my door. I looked at my wrist-watch. Ten minutes past four.

I opened the door. There was a big fat man standing there. He had on about three hundred bucks' worth of clothes. His fat cheeks hung down over a stiff white collar, and his wide face was red and smoothly shaven. Large gray eyes peered at me from beneath bushy black brows. He was wearing a pin-striped dark gray suit. A heavy gold watch-chain was stretched across his bulging pin-striped paunch, and he wore a soft gray felt hat with the brim turned up all around.

"Yeah?" I said.

"Mr. Bennett?" he asked.

His voice was deep and rich.

I said, "Yeah" again.

He hesitated.

"Ah—may I come in? For a moment?"

"Look," I said. "It's after four o'clock in the morning."

He bowed slightly.

"I wish to apologize for the lateness of the hour. But it's very important that I speak to you."

I felt nasty.

"Important to whom, you?"

He didn't get sore. He smiled and spread his fat, well-kept hands in a soothing gesture.

"To both of us."

I GRUNTED and stepped aside. After all, my night's sleep was ruined anyhow and I admit that I was a little curious. He lumbered through the doorway and I motioned him to a chair. He sat down with a sigh and extracted a fat cigar from a long silver case.

He bit off the end of the cigar, and applied flame with a silver lighter. Then he said, "Pardon me," and offered me a cigar. I shook my head and lit a cigarette. He took off his hat and laid it on the table beside him. Thin graying hair was meticulously parted over his pink skull. He sighed again and exhaled a vast cloud of smoke. I waited.

"Mr. Bennett," he said. "I'll come directly to the point. I know all about you, who you are, who you work for. You have interested yourself in the affairs of the Haynes Truck Lines. Am I right?"

I shrugged.

"You're telling it."

He spread his hands again.

"All right. Please don't think it's flattery when I say that I know your reputation. I've come here to suggest, shall we say, a business proposition?"

He paused and looked up at me from under his bushy brows.

"How much?" I asked.

He laughed and spread his hands.

"That's what I like. I like a man who comes right to the point."

He laid his cigar in an ash tray and withdrew a wallet from his inside coat pocket. He opened it and his thick white fingers extracted a sheaf of crisp new one-hundred-dollar bills. He counted out five bills and tossed them on the table in front of me. He motioned with his hand, palm up.

"For what?" I said.

He laughed again, a rich, deep laugh from way down.

"Now, now, Mr. Bennett."

Then he sighed deeply, picked up his cigar and stuck it between his teeth. When he spoke again his voice had lost its smoothness, and its gaiety.

"You ask, for what? For this. Stay away from the Haynes Truck Lines. Do not concern yourself in the least—in the least—with their affairs at the present time. That's all."

"Not for five hundred bucks," I said.

He looked at me steadily for perhaps thirty seconds. Then he clamped his teeth tighter on his cigar and took out his wallet again. He counted out five more one-hundred-dollar bills and laid them on top of the first five. He looked up at me, his cigar in his teeth. He didn't speak.

I picked up the ten crisp bills, folded them once and stuck them in my pants' pocket.

"Okay," I said.

He pushed himself to his feet, flicked a cigar ash from his vest, walked to the door. I followed him. At the door he turned.

"Do we understand each other?" he asked politely.

"Sure," I said.

"Mr. Bennett," he said. "I'm very glad to hear you say that. For my sake—and yours."

I grinned at him, my hand on the bills in my pocket.

"You don't have to get tough. A deal's a deal."

He nodded.

"Very well. Good night, Mr. Bennett."

He went out and closed the door.

I locked the door behind him. The odor of his cigar was heavy in the room. I opened the windows wide, undressed and got into bed. In two minutes I was asleep. I dreamed about a young fellow lying on a slab at the De Lancey Funeral Home. In my dream the young fellow suddenly sat up straight and pointed an accusing finger at me.

CHAPTER TWO
DEATH FREIGHT

I GOT up about eleven, showered, shaved, and put on my other suit. Then I called the office, learned that the Boss was still down south and wouldn't be back until the week-end. I told his secretary that I had finished the West Coast job and that my report was in the mail. She said that the Boss had left no instructions. She would call me as soon as he came back. That suited me fine.

I went down to the dining room and got on the outside of two eggs, a slab of ham, about a quart of orange juice and three cups of coffee. After that I went out, snagged a taxi, told the driver to take me to the main terminal of the Haynes Truck Lines. When I got there Art was just going out to lunch so I went along and drank bourbon and soda while he ate. We talked about a lot of things, and he went over the whole story with me again. It was going on two o'clock when we got back to Art's office.

"Sit down," Art said. "I've got a couple of phone calls to make."

He sat down behind his desk and began to scribble on a pad.

"I think I'll amble over to the freight depot and nose around a little," I said. "I'll come back and pick you up in time for the loading of the car."

I heard a car stop in the driveway outside. I was standing by the window, and Art's desk was almost in a line with me.

"Okay," Art said, and then I heard the sound of gunfire.

The glass splintered behind me, and I yelled to Art and pitched forward to the floor. I lay there, hugging the rug. There were three shots, and then I heard the whine of gears as the car outside roared away. I lifted my head.

Art was slumped over his desk, and blood was running in a bright stream over the green blotter. I ran over to him. The lapels of his tan gabardine suit and the collar of his white shirt were stained red.

A wide-eyed, white-faced girl came running in from an adjoining office and stood staring.

"Call a doctor," I snapped, and she disappeared.

I lifted Art out of the chair and stretched him out on the floor.

"What the blazes, Jim?" he said, and opened his eyes.

"Shut up," I ordered. "Take it easy."

In a minute the office was filled with truck drivers, mechanics and office help. I waved them all out and locked the door. I got Art's coat off him, and cut off his shirt with a pair of shears which I found on his desk. He had been hit once. The slug had gone through the flesh at the base of his neck just over his collar bone.

There came a pounding on the door. I opened it. It was the doctor. He got to work on Art, and I looked at my watch. Twenty minutes past two.

"You'll be okay," I said to Art. "I'm going over to the freight depot. See you later."

He grinned up at me.

"Okay, Jim. Take my car. Keys are in it."

"All right," I said. "Take it easy."

OUTSIDE, I got into Art's blue job, and headed across town. It was a quarter of three when I pulled up outside the freight depot. I went out to the loading platform. There were three trucks backed up to the dock unloading their cargo into the freight car. Two of the trucks belonged to the Haynes Truck Lines. I spotted a tall blond young fellow standing by. He had a scar over his right eye, and his nose was flat.

I moved over and stood beside him.

"You Orville Westover's brother?" I asked him.

He looked at me.

"Yeah. Who are you?"

"A friend of Haynes'. He sent me over to watch the loading. You going along in the car?"

"Yeah."

"I'm sorry about your brother," I said. "Why don't you forget this ride for a couple of days?"

I didn't know what the kid was letting himself in for, and I had a hunch that I ought to try and keep him from going.

"Hold off a couple of days." I continued. "Maybe we'll turn up something."

"I'm going—now."

I shrugged. "You got a rod?"

He spat on the platform.

"Blast it, no."

I turned my back on the loading gang, slipped my .38 out my pocket, and handed it to him.

"You better take this."

"Thanks," he said, "but I won't need it." He held up a fist. "This'll be enough."

There was an ugly glint in his eyes.

"Look," I said, "don't be a sap. Whoever bumped off your brother—if he was bumped off—wasn't fooling. You may be tough, but if you get stumped between here and Detroit you'll need more than your dukes."

He spat again.

"I ain't worried. When they open that door, I'll be ready for 'em."

I shrugged again.

"Okay. But keep your eyes open—all of the time."

He didn't answer me. He walked away and began to talk to the freight agent who was standing by preparing to seal the car as soon as it was loaded. I looked around. The two Haynes' trucks were almost empty and I saw hauled into the car the last of a number of small cases marked for a tool company in Detroit.

I went over to the freight agent and nodded at the cases.

"Diamond tool bits?"

The agent was a thin man with a gray mustache. He looked at me sharply.

"Why?" he asked, wary.

"Just wondered."

He walked away, the big blond kid following him. In a minute the agent was back. He had a beefy man with him.

"That's him," the agent said, and pointed at me.

The beefy man stepped up close, opened his coat and flashed a shiny badge on me.

"Wilkens," he said. "Police Department."

"My, my," I said.

"Don't get smart. What're you doing here?"

"Just looking," I said.

"Why you asking about them tool bits?"

"Curious," I said. "I hear they're worth a lot of dough."

"Yeah," said the beefy man. He grabbed my arm. "You better come along with me."

"Go away," I said. "I'm working for Haynes." I showed him my agency card.

"Jim Bennett." I said.

"Why didn't you say so?" he snapped.

He looked hurt.

"You didn't ask me."

He gave me a sidelong glance, shifted his feet. "How do you figure this thing?"

"I don't. Just getting the layout."

"Got any ideas?"

"A couple," I lied. "They may be cold."

He shifted his feet again, gave me another sidelong glance.

"Why, ah, what kind of ideas?" he asked.

"Oh," I said. "This and that."

I was watching the loaders. The car was just about filled. Through the open doors I could see eight or ten bales of copper wire, a half dozen big wooden boxes labeled HANDLE WITH CARE—GRINDING WHEELS, a huge rope necklace of brass plumbing fixtures, and other odds and ends of freight.

Three men sweated and wrestled a crated piano through the doors and the car was filled. The agent peered inside, and began to handle his metal seals and wire. I looked at my watch and saw that it was a couple of minutes of three. The agent said "All right" to the big blond kid, and the kid nodded and stepped into the car.

The agent turned over one of the cases of tool bits, and the kid sat down on it. When they shut the doors he wouldn't have much room for his three-hour ride to

Detroit. The Agent said something to the kid, and the kid laughed. Then he nodded his head and the agent closed the doors and applied his sealing apparatus.

I watched very carefully, and I saw that it would be impossible to open those doors without breaking the seal. Then he went around to the other side, and I followed him. He sealed the opposite doors in the same manner.

The agent came back to the platform, waved his arms, and went into his office. Up ahead I heard the toot of the locomotive, and the cars banged together all along the line. The train began to move.

THE BEEFY dick was watching the train, and I took the opportunity to duck into the agent's office. He was sorting bills of lading at a high desk. I showed him my agency card, told him again that I was working for Haynes, asked if he could give me some information. He said, sure, if he could.

"Thanks," I said. "I'll admit that right now I'm just fishing around. I came on this job cold. But it might help—and it might not—if I knew the contents of each car when the Haynes stuff was stolen. Can you give me that?"

He scratched his head.

"I dunno. That's a pretty big order. When would you have to have it?"

"Now."

"Afraid I can't right now. Maybe tomorrow if I ain't too busy."

"Okay," I said. "I'll be back tomorrow. But right now, think back. Can you tell me, from memory, some of the items which were on the cars with the Haynes' stuff?"

"Well," he said, "Maybe I can remember some of the big things. We been shipping a lot of copper wire to Detroit, lots of grinding wheels, airplane parts, and of course, the tools, bits and stuff for Haynes, a piano once in a while, lots of big castings, electric motors—that's about all I can think of off hand. Does that help?"

"Not much," I said. "That's heavy stuff. Grinding wheels, for example. Where do they come from?"

The agent thumbed through his papers.

"Haynes trucks them up from the factory south of Akron," he explained. "Ohio Abrasives Company."

I made a mental note of the name of the company. "Okay. Now, who ships the pianos?"

He did some more thumbing.

"Clear-Tone Piano Company, here in Cleveland."

He gave me an address on the east side, out past 105th Street.

I couldn't think of anything else to ask him, and then I had an idea.

"Does that freight make any stops between here and Detroit?"

"Nope. Fast freight. Straight through—except in an emergency."

"Have you had any emergency stops lately?"

"Look, mister. A lot of trains go through here in a day."

"You don't know if any stops were made?"

"Heck, no."

I laid a five-dollar bill on his desk.

"Thanks. I'll be back tomorrow. Try and have that list ready."

I went out, climbed into Art's convertible, and headed up town. I had gone about six blocks, when I had an idea. I began to sweat. I thought of that kid on the car headed for Detroit, and I pulled into the first parking place I found.

I sat behind the wheel and tried to figure things out. The more I thought about the whole business the more I began to sweat. But I had to be sure. I put the car in gear, made a U turn, hoping that no traffic cops were around, and headed east. I swung into Carnegie and kept going until I hit 105th Street. Then I began looking.

I finally found it. It was a small room sandwiched between a barber shop and a second-hand furniture store. The barber shop was closed. On the windows of the address I wanted were crude letters notifying anyone interested that this was the home of "The Clear-Tone Piano Company. Office and Sales Room."

I looked through the smudged glass windows but I couldn't see any pianos, although there were several piano crates standing along one wall. I also saw a stack of white bags which looked as though they might contain anything from flour to cement. I transferred my .38 to my right-hand coat pocket and went in.

The place smelled musty and only dim light trickled in through the dirty front windows. If they did any business at all here, I couldn't see it.

A medium-sized man got up from a small shabby desk in the corner and came toward me. He wore rimless eyeglasses, and had thick white hair and a thin white mustache. His gray tweed suit was well tailored.

"Good afternoon," he said.

I stood about three feet from the door and I knew I could make it to the sidewalk in five seconds if I had to. I kept my hand on the gun in my pocket.

"I want to buy a piano," I said.

The white-haired man looked me over very carefully. Then he said, very politely. "Yes, sir. Will you wait a moment? I'll call Mr. Darmody."

He made a move toward a door opening into a back room.

"Stand still," I ordered sharply.

He stood still, watching me. I kept one eye on him, and one eye on the back-room door. From beyond the door I heard a slight sound. The white-haired man heard it, too. His eyes flicked toward the door, but he didn't move. The place was silent again, but I could hear the sound of traffic outside in the street. It sounded far away, and I suddenly felt very lonely.

CHAPTER THREE
BLOOD ON THE PIANO

A MAN came through the backroom doorway. He was a big man in a dark pin-striped suit, with a heavy watch chain across his paunch. He moved ponderously through the door and stopped just beyond it. He was holding a fat cigar in one white hand. His other hand was jingling silver in his pants pocket.

"Well, Bennett," he said, "have you come to return the thousand dollars?"

"No," I said. "Mr. Darmody—is that it?—we're even on that—after your play at Haynes' office this afternoon."

He sighed deeply.

"The boys didn't do so well. Maybe we should give them another chance."

He turned his head sideward, toward the back room.

"George," he called in a soft voice.

The white-haired man standing at my left suddenly jumped backward and his right hand darted to his inside coat pocket. In the same instant a gun roared from behind the back-room partition. I heard the slug smash the glass door behind me.

I cut loose with the .38 in my coat pocket, right through the cloth of my second best suit, and the white-haired man hit the floor, his legs twitching. I ducked down and tried to watch the fat man and at the same time tried to figure out where the shooting was coming from behind the partition.

I ran, stooping, away from the door, and the unseen gun barked again. I heard the splatter of splinters from the spot on the floor about where I had been standing. But now I had spotted a small square hole in the wall to the right of the back room door, and I cleared the gun from pocket and let fly at it.

I heard a sobbing yelp from behind the partition. The fat man started to curse in a high, shrill voice. His fat hands were clenched out in front of him, like a movie heroine at a horse race, and he stood with his knees bent, springing his big body up and down.

"You fools! You fools!" he screamed. "Come in and get him!"

I heard a pounding of feet from the back room, and I figured it was time for me to fade. The fat man was apparently not carrying a rod, so I let him be. I jerked open the glass-splintered door and as I did so I heard a gun roar behind me. Something socked me on the head, and I hit the sidewalk, face first.

I scrambled up, my feet slipping on the cement, and made it to the car. People were running from all directions. Automatically I went through the motions of starting the car. The motor roared out, and I highballed out of there.

Things were a little hazy, but I knew I was driving all right. The back of my neck felt wet and sticky, and my hand felt kind of numb, but all I could think of was that blond kid sealed in the freight car on his way to Detroit. Ten blocks away I pulled up in front of a drug store, climbed out and went in, dabbing at my neck and head with a handkerchief.

I found a phone booth, called Police Headquarters, and asked for Detective Wilkens.

"This is Bennett," I said, when I got him on the wire. "Take four or five of the boys and go over to the Clear-Tone Piano Company, on the east side, south of 105th. You'll find one stiff and one probable—if they haven't hauled them away. Good-bye."

I heard him say "Hey—" before I hung up. Then I called Art Haynes' house, but before I got an answer the phone booth got dark and began to spin around in circles. I left the receiver dangling and started for the street and some fresh air. But I never made it. I remember hanging onto a stool in front of the soda fountain. I had hold of the stool with both hands and it kept turning and my head got lower and lower.

Very plainly I could see the checker-board linoleum and the litter of cigarette butts and matches beneath the stool. Then I fell off the stool, and rolled over or my back. A woman began screaming. I thought of the blond kid in the freight car again, and I could hear the woman screaming. I went out cold then with the scream ringing in my ears.

WHEN I opened my eyes again I was in bed. A high narrow bed and a girl dressed in white with a white cap on her black hair was standing at the foot of it. She was folding some clothes over her arm, and I recognized my blue second best suit.

The girl was short with chubby cheeks, long black eyelashes and too much lipstick.

"Honey, give me my pants," I said, and sat up.

My head hurt and I felt kind of dizzy, but otherwise okay. I put my hand to my head and I felt a gob of gauze and tape above my left ear.

The girl looked at me startled.

"Give 'em to me," I said. "I gotta go."

She began backing away, and I swung my feet to the floor. They had put a short nightgown on me which came to my knees, and I felt a little silly. But all I could think of was that I had to get dressed and get out there, and fast. I started for the girl. The room began to tilt sideward, but I kept going. I grabbed the clothes from her hands, sat down in a chair beside the bed, and began to put on my socks.

For the first time I noticed that there were a lot of other beds in the room, and the men in them were all looking at me. I put on my shoes, then my shorts, and pulled the nightgown over my head. Once I had to wait for the room to stop spinning, but I made it. When I came to my necktie, I put it in my pocket. I put on my coat, made sure that my wallet and gun were still in it, and started for the door.

"Mister, you aren't supposed to leave yet," the girl said.

"Okay, okay."

I fished my wrist-watch out my coat pocket, strapped it on, looked at the time. The hands stood at six-thirty. Something was wrong. I looked at the girl.

"What time you got?"

She glanced at her wrist.

"Six-twenty-eight. Mister, you can't leave. I'll get in trouble. Dr. Hammerstein—"

"What time did they bring me in here?" She looked at a chart on the foot of the bed.

"Four-o-five this afternoon. I'll call Dr. Hammer—"

"Okay. Call him. Tell him I said thanks. You, too."

I tossed some bills on the bed, grabbed my hat, and went out the door. I found the elevator, went down, and hit the street. Nobody stopped me. The fresh air felt good. I walked a block before I nabbed a taxi.

"Airport," I said, climbing in and settling back in the seat.

The cushions felt soft and restful, and I leaned my head back. All I could think about was that kid in the freight car, no stops, straight through to Detroit. He'd be there by now, maybe, and I knew that I had to get there quick. Maybe I was all wrong. I hoped so.

I thought about Art Haynes, about the slug he had stopped, the slug which had been intended for me, and about the young fellow on the slab at the De Lancey Funeral Home, about the kid on the freight car. I knew I'd catch blazes from the Boss for going on a job without telling him, but I was in this thing now, fee or no fee, and I was going to see it through to the end. My head throbbed with every bump of the taxi, but it wasn't too bad.

At the airport I found that there was a plane leaving for Detroit in twenty minutes. They fussed around about giving me a seat, but I talked fast, showed them my agency card, told them that I was working for Haynes, and they finally sold me a ticket. After that I went out to a phone booth, called Art's house. His wife answered.

"Jim!" she exclaimed. "Where've you been? We want you here for dinner."

"Alice," I said. "I'll take a rain check on that. I'm leaving for Detroit in ten minutes. How's Art?"

"All right, Jim. He says he's going back to work tomorrow."

"That's good," I said. "Tell him to sit tight. I'll see him when I get back."

She started to protest, but I said, "Good-by, Alice," and hung up. Every time I saw Art and his wife I began to feel sorry for myself, and I would tell myself that I was going to get out of the racket and settle down and live like decent people. But I never did.

I had two more phone calls to make. I hated to make the first one because I knew what I would find out. I called the manager of the Detroit terminal of the Haynes Truck Lines, and I listened almost wearily while his excited voice told me what I feared. If that slug hadn't nicked my head and put me out for a couple of hours, I might have had time to do something about the kid in the freight car. But it was too late now to do anything for him.

The manager in Detroit gave it to me fast. The car had arrived, the seals intact, but Haynes' shipment of tool bits and micrometers was gone—and Pete Westover was gone, too. He ended by saying that he had called the Cleveland terminal but that they had told him that Mr. Haynes had been hurt.

"Yeah," I said, "but not bad. You take it easy. I'm leaving for Detroit in a couple of minutes."

AFTER THAT I called the freight office, got them to give me the consignee of the piano they had shipped to Detroit that afternoon. I wrote it down and went over to the airport restaurant. I had time for a sandwich and two cups of black coffee before my plane came in. When the big Mainliner stopped rolling over the cement I was the first one in line.

It didn't take us long to get to Detroit, but it seemed like a long ride to me. I got into a taxi at the airport, told the driver to take me to The White Music Company and I gave him the address. It took us almost a half hour, but we finally found it a few blocks off John R. way out. It was a dingy building on the corner of an alley. No lights were showing, and the whole neighborhood was dark.

"You want to wait?" I said to the driver.

He looked around at the dark buildings. "I don't know, Jack," he said. "How long you gonna be?"

"Not long, I hope. How much is the fare?"

He looked at the meter.

"Three seventy."

"Okay," I said. "Here's twenty bucks. How about waiting ten minutes?"

He took the twenty.

"Ten minutes," he said.

I opened the door, got to the sidewalk.

"Leave your motor running—and the door open."

He looked at me. He was a little fellow with a long nose and a scraggly mustache.

"It's like that, huh?" he said.

He looked scared.

"Don't worry," I said. "Stick around."

I went down the alley, not making any noise. A sagging board fence ran from the rear of the building back to another cross alley. I stooped down behind the fence and scooted around to the back. The fence ran across to the adjoining building, but I saw the hinges of a wide gate. It was padlocked. I went back around the alley to the rear of the building again, grabbed the top of the fence and hoisted myself over.

I landed on a pile of trash—rusty cans, empty crates, and I don't know what all. I made quite a bit of noise. I ducked over to the building and squatted down in the deep shadow.

I waited a minute or two. Nothing happened. I felt my way along the rear of the building until I came to a window.

It was nailed shut, and at first I couldn't see a thing through the dirty glass. And then I made out the faint glimmer of a light from inside the building, but I couldn't see anything else.

I decided that the light must be shining through a crack from an inner room. I backed away from the window, and looked around me. My eyes were becoming a little accustomed to the darkness and for the first time I saw the bulky outline of a truck parked at the far end of the building. I sneaked over to it and looked around.

The cab was empty. I walked around to the back, climbed up into the rear, over the chained-up end gate. It was very dark, and I waited a minute before I started to crawl forward. I moved slowly on my hands and knees. My groping hands struck a solid object, and I felt over its surface and slowly got to my feet. I was standing beside a big wooden box with a half slanting surface. I didn't need a light to tell me that it was the kind of a box in which upright pianos are shipped.

I lit a match and carefully shielded the flame with my hands. One of the top boards of the box was loosely nailed, and I pulled it loose with one hand. One end came away, but the other end stuck. I looked more closely and saw that it was held to the box on the inside by a hook, the kind commonly used on screen doors. Then I saw that there was a hook on the other side, too. I felt along the top of the box and my fingers encountered two holes, about an inch in diameter, bored into the wood.

The match went out then, and I went to work in the dark. I felt down on the inside of the box through the opening I had made in the top. There were hooks on the inside holding the second board in place. I pulled the hooks out of the eyes and lifted the board out. I now had a good-sized opening, and I reached in as far as I could and felt around.

Nothing. The box was apparently empty. But as I stood close to the opening I had made, an odor came out of the box, an odor which was too familiar to me—a sweetish smell which I had encountered often. It was the smell of blood.

I lit another match. A thin semi-liquid puddle had seeped from a crack in the box onto the truck floor. Still holding the match I poked my head into the opening at the top of the box. Huddled at the bottom was the body of a man. His legs were drawn up, and his head was doubled down against his chest. The top of his head was a red soggy smear. But I could see enough of the face to recognize the flattened nose of Pete Westover.

CHAPTER FOUR
CONCERTO FOR BULLETS

THE MATCH burned my fingers and I dropped it. I took a deep breath. The thing to do was to get the devil out of there and to the nearest police station. I had found what I had dreaded to find. There was nothing more I could do. Both Westover brothers were dead—murdered within two days.

But I felt that if I had been a little quicker on the trigger, the second death wouldn't have been necessary. I started for the rear of the truck hoping that my taxi was still waiting.

And then I heard a sound, a faint, bubbling sound and I stopped. It was coming from the box, and I knew that Pete Westover still lived. I listened and I could hear his faint irregular breathing. I knew what I had to do—get out of there, get help, and come back.

I started for the rear of the truck, but before I gone two steps I heard voices, and the sound of a door being softly closed. I didn't want to be cornered on the truck so I made a leap for the end gate, climbed to the ground, and ducked around to the side of the truck next to the fence.

I had an idea then. I took out my pocket knife, opened the largest blade and ripped a dandy hole in the truck's left rear tire. But I hadn't counted on the noise the escaping air would make. The loud hissing sounded to my ears as shrill as the wail of a police siren. I heard a low exclamation from the front of the truck and the sound of footsteps on the cinders.

I leaped for the fence. But I wasn't quick enough. They came at me from both sides of the truck. Two of them, one from each end. I didn't have time to unlimber my .38. As they closed in, I hung on to the top of the fence and let fly with both feet. My heel got one of them square in the stomach. He grunted and fell back against the side of the truck.

The other one came on in. I used both feet on him, in the vicinity of his nose and mouth, and he went down beneath the truck. But when I kicked at him I lost my hold on the top of the fence. I fell into the weeds. I got my .38 in my hand then, and started to rise. As I did so, I saw a shadowy bulk standing beside the truck's cab. I also saw the dull gleam of what I knew was a gun And then I saw something else.

The first man I had kicked was crawling slowly toward me in the darkness. The other one was stretched out nice and still beneath the truck. I crouched down in the weeds and pressed my back against the fence, brought up my .38. I was pretty sure that the man standing by the cab couldn't see me. If he could see me, I figured he was trying to make up his mind whether or not I was one of his pals. But I had to do something. The man on my right was still wriggling toward me.

I yelled as loud as I could and made a dive beneath the truck. In the same instant I let the crawling man have it point blank with my .38. He stopped crawling and rolled over on his back. Almost instantly the gun in the hand of the man by the cab spat orange flame and I heard the thud of the slug as it hit the cinders beside me.

I flopped over on my stomach and let fly in the direction of the cab. But the man who had been standing there was gone. I figured he was hiding behind the front wheels of the truck, and so I lay still and watched.

One of the guys I had kicked was lying close beside me. He began to show signs of coming around, and so I smacked my gun against his head. He lay still again. I crawled, snake fashion to the other side of the truck and cautiously looked out. Over here, away from the shadow of the fence, I could see better. I made out the form of a man crouching behind the front wheel. I propped myself on one elbow, held my gun out in front of me, and took a better look.

EVEN IN the darkness the shape of the man was familiar. I guess it was the turned-up hat brim. He made a good target, but I have never been very good at shooting people when they aren't looking—even a killer like Darmody. It's silly of me, and it has sent me into unnecessary trouble more than once. But that's the way I am.

"Darmody," I said, softly.

He whirled sideward, instantly, and I saw the bright flash of his gun. And even as I pressed the trigger of my own gun I felt a sudden hot hammer-like blow on my left forearm. But I stayed propped on my right elbow and I squeezed the trigger of the .38 four times. Darmody flung violently backward, away from the wheel, and sprawled on his back in the open. His gun was still in his hand and as he hit the ground it exploded, the flame from the muzzle pointing straight at the starless sky. He lay still after that, a huge, grunting bulk in the shadows.

I started to crawl out from under the truck, but a sudden roar of gunfire from the dark doorway of the building caused me to duck my head back under again. What the devil? I thought. Cleveland and Detroit both ganging up on me? But I didn't hang around to think about it.

I emptied my gun at the doorway, and under cover of this barrage I scooted over to the fence, made the top in one leap, and dropped into the alley on the other side. Staccato reports came from the building, and splinters flew from along the top of the fence. I ran down the alley, stooping as low as I could, and holding my injured arm.

I got a break. The taxi was still waiting. When the driver saw me coming he put the cab in gear and started to move it slowly along the curb. I jumped onto the running-board, climbed into the front seat and before I had the door closed we were almost to the next block. I looked back and I could see the lights coming on all over the neighborhood, and close by I heard the shrill sound of policeman's whistle.

"Take it easy," I said. "Nobody's chasing you.

For the first time the cab driver looked at me.

"Jeepers, Jack! I thought you was never coming! Hey, they got you!"

"Not bad," I said. "Nicked my arm. Go to the nearest police station."

"Okay, Jack. You a cop?"

"No," I said. "Junior G-Man. Weasel patrol."

"Cripes!"

The cops at the station treated me okay. I showed them my agency card, and the fact that I had a couple of friends on the Detroit force helped quite a bit. My head was hurting, and my arm didn't feel too good, but I managed to give them a quick picture of what was going on and they sent a work crew over to the music company office off John R. I stayed at the station.

They fixed up my arm, changed the dressing on the bullet groove in my head, got me a room at a downtown hotel, and took me there in a squad car. I thanked the boys, went in and registered, had two drinks at the bar, and went up to my room. As soon as I hit the bed I was asleep.

In the morning I took a cab to police headquarters. I introduced myself to the chief, told him of my part in the previous night's doings.

"We made a good haul, thanks to you, Bennett," he said, when I got through. "We cleaned out the whole rat's nest. All of them had records. When the boys got out there two of them were just pulling out in the truck. They made a run for it, and we had to stop them. The driver was killed, the other one is in the hospital. The boy in the piano box was still living. He had a fractured skull, but the hospital reports that he is doing all right this morning. Going to pull out of it okay."

I sighed. I felt kind of responsible for Pete Westover, and it was good news to me.

"What about the rest of them?" I asked.

"One of them was dead—lying behind the building where you dropped him. Another was walking around in a daze. He had a broken nose, and all of his front teeth were knocked out. What did you hit him with—a crowbar?"

"What about Darmody—the fat man?"

"Darmody? We knew him as Julian Mitchell—anyhow, that's one of his names. He had two slugs in his middle, one in his chest. He may live. We've wanted him for a long time."

"What for?"

"Different things—blackmail, manslaughter, hi-jacking. He ran the gang—been operating all along the Lake."

"Did you find any of the Haynes' stuff?"

"Yeah. Lots of it. Mostly tool bits, precision tools, stuff like that. All big money stuff."

"That'll make Art Haynes feel good. You'll probably be hearing from him."

CAREFULLY THE chief lit a big black cigar. "How did you get next to the outfit?" he asked.

"I hafta go," I said, "but I'll give it to you fast. I checked with the railroad in Cleveland and found that every time they had a loss there was an upright piano in the shipment. I did some more checking, learned that the gang was using a phony piano company gag to get a piano box on the freight car. They had a pretty good racket. They loaded the piano box with bags of sand to give it the right weight and left enough room for a man to stand inside it. Then they'd put one of their boys in the box, leave a couple of holes in the top for air.

"The front boards of the box were held in place with hooks—from the inside. Then they would haul it down to the station at the last minute so that it would be one of the last pieces of freight loaded—so that it wouldn't be buried in the back of the car behind a lot of other stuff.

"After the car was loaded, sealed, and on its way, the man inside the box would let himself out, empty the sand bags through the lower crack of the freight car door, push the empty bags out, and then take what he wanted inside the car and put it in the piano box, fasten himself in again and wait for his pals to carry him out at the end of the line.

"The two Westover boys were apparently looking for trouble at the time the car was unloaded. It cost one of them his life. They didn't suspect that anything would happen while the car was in transit. It was easy for the fellow inside the box to tell that they were in the car. He would watch his chance, maybe wait until they fell asleep, and then let himself out of the box and shug them.

"Things were pretty hot after the first killing, and so the second time they got rid of the body by piling it in with the loot. I figure that both of the Westover boys were slugged with an oversize blackjack—maybe a sash cord weight. Pete Westover was lucky—they didn't hit him hard enough."

"The stiff we found in the alley had a big blackjack on him," the chief said. "He was a little feller—could easily hide in a piano box. He might have been the lad they used."

"I hope so," I said.

The chief asked me to give his regards to the Boss, we talked a little more, and then I left. I took a cab to the Haynes Detroit terminal and bummed a ride on the next outfit headed for Cleveland. I settled down in the cab and went to sleep while we were going through Dearborn, and I didn't wake up until we unloaded at Toledo. We pulled into Cleveland late in the afternoon. When I walked into Art's office he was sitting at his desk. He had on a tan sport shirt open at the throat, and I could see the bandage around his neck. Otherwise he looked okay.

"Thanks for the free ride," I said. "A little bumpy, but not bad."

"For Pete's sake," exclaimed Art. "I was just getting ready to call the cops."

"I'm afraid it's all over now, including the shooting," I said.

He stared at me wonderingly.

"Give," he said. "Don't keep me in suspense."

"Sure."

He got out the bourbon, and I gave him the whole story.

"By the way," he said, when I had finished, "there was a dick named Wilkens looking for you. Said something about going out to a piano company, and that there was nobody there."

"I was afraid of that," I said. "That's why I went to Detroit."

"You did a good job," said Art. "Even if I did stop a bullet intended for you."

"Don't thank me," I said. "The Boss will send you a bill." I got up, picked up my hat. "Me for a shower, shave, then dinner."

"Quit hinting," Art said. "You're coming out to my place. Alice promised to have a batch of Manhattans waiting for us—if and when you got back."

"Fine," I said. "You can wait for me while I clean up. Let's go."

As we started for the door, I suddenly remembered something. I stopped, took out my wallet, and counted out the ten one hundred dollar bills which Darmody had given me. I handed them to Art.

"Here. This belongs to Orville Westover's widow and kids. Will you see that they get it?"

Art looked at me.

"Sure," he said. "Old hard-boiled Jim."

He took the money and locked it in his office safe.

When we got out to Art's place his wife kissed me, and the Manhattans were swell. So was the dinner.

KILLERS CAN'T BE CARELESS

TURN A BIG-CITY DICK LOOSE IN THE WOODED HILLS OF OHIO, SHOOT AT HIM FROM ALL DIRECTIONS, AND WHAT DO YOU HAVE? A PRIVATE EYE SEEING RED! JIM BENNETT DIDN'T LIKE TO SERVE AS A TARGET, BUT IT WAS EVEN MORE MADDENING TO BE TAKEN FOR A DUMMY, AND WHEN HE GOT THE RANGE, THE SLICKEST HICK IN THE HILLS DIDN'T HAVE A CHANCE AGAINST HIM.

CHAPTER ONE
A HUNTING WE WILL GO

SANDY HOLLIS was a good secretary. Not only that, she was easy to look at. She had reddish-brown hair, a short straight nose and long handsome legs. One day in November she said to me: "Jim, do you like to hunt?"

I wiped the oil from the .38 I was cleaning, and asked: "Man or beast?"

"Neither. Birds—ring-necked pheasants."

"Sure, I said. "I'll use my .38."

"Quit bragging," she laughed. "Even James Tobais Bennett, the famous private investigator, can't hit a pheasant with a .38—unless it was sitting. And you don't shoot sitting birds."

"Tell me more," I said, as I dropped cartridges into the cylinder of my freshly cleaned gun.

She pushed her chair back from her desk and crossed her good-looking legs. "I had a letter from Dad. He says there are a lot of birds on the place this fall. He wants me to come down for some shooting. Dad's got plenty of guns, and Mom's fried chicken is super, and Ralph will be there, and some other people."

"Who's Ralph?" I asked. "The boy friend?"

I shouldn't have said it. I knew that Sandy didn't have a boy friend—not yet. Her young husband was too freshly buried on the beach at Tarawa.

Her eyes sobered for just an instant, and then she laughed. "You know better, Jim. Ralph is my brother—

The ashcan moved very slightly, with a small scraping sound. Then the narrow alley roared and shook with gunfire.

he's just back from Tokyo. He's been in the Pacific since Iwo Jima."

"Sounds like a family affair," I said. "Why should I butt in?"

"Look," she said, "you haven't had much fun lately—and I want the folks to see what a swell boss I've got."

It sounded good. For a long time I hadn't done anything but chase people on the wrong side of the law, and I suddenly realized that I hadn't had any fun for months. Sandy's invitation was very attractive.

I put my gun in a desk drawer, got up and put on my hat and coat.

"Where are you going?" Sandy asked.

"Out to buy a hunting license," I said, "and some regulation hunting clothes—red coat, high boots, a plaid shirt. You know, tally-ho."

Sandy said: "Swell." She really sounded pleased. "We leave tomorrow afternoon."

THE HOLLIS farm was about a hundred miles southwest of Cleveland, and we drove into the well-kept barn yard at five-thirty in the afternoon. Sandy's father came around a corner of one of the out-buildings. He took off his heavy gloves to shake hands with me. He was a tall, lean, friendly man, with a thin weather-beaten face and kind blue eyes.

"Please, Mr. Bennett," he said. "Sandy has written us a lot about you."

"Call me Jim," I said.

"All right—if you'll call me Homer." He smiled shyly.

"A deal," I said, and the three of us walked across the neat back lawn to the screened-in summer kitchen adjoining the rear of the house. A short plump woman came out of the kitchen door wiping her hands on her apron.

"Mom, this is Mr. Bennett, Sandy's boss," Homer Hollis said.

Her pleasant flushed face lit up, and I took her moist hand. And then we were in the kitchen. There was the warm smell of roasting chicken and baking biscuits. They led me through the big house and into a long living room where the flames from a fireplace crackled pleasantly and filled the room with a flickering light. There were comfortable furniture, occasional rugs, bare polished hardwood floors, a grand piano. Through long wide windows I could see across a sweep of lawn, and the white highway at the end of the lane showed up faintly in the dusk. As I watched, the lights of a car turned into the lane.

Mrs. Hollis peered out the window. "Here comes Ralph and Eileen," she said.

"Mom, how has he been?" Sandy asked.

"All right, I guess," she replied. "But he's thin—and kind of restless."

"They all are at first," Sandy said. "When are he and Eileen going to get married?"

Her mother shrugged her plump shoulders. "You ask him, Sandy. He don't seem to want to tell us anything."

Sandy laughed. "After all, Mom, *he's* the one who's getting married." She took her mother's arm. "Come on, I'll help you get the chicken up. Sit down, Jim, and relax. I've got a surprise for you." They left the room.

I sat down, but I didn't relax very long. I heard shouting and laughter in the kitchen, and then Sandy came back into the living room. With her was a tall, lean dark young man, and a small blond girl.

And so I met Ralph Hollis, late Lieutenant Hollis, of the U.S. Army, and his pretty bride-to-be, Eileen Fortune. He was pleasant and quiet, and Eileen hung on to his arm as though she would never let him go. And then Sandy brought in a big pitcher of Manhattan cocktails, a tray of glasses and a bowl of cherries.

"This is the surprise, Jim," she said. "You didn't think we served cocktails out here in the sticks, did you?"

"It must be a special occasion," Ralph said, and grinned. "I never saw a cocktail in this house before I went away."

"Two special occasions." Sandy laughed. "You're home, and my boss is here."

"She'll probably ask me for a raise Monday," I said to Ralph.

Homer Hollis came into the room. He had put on a dark suit, and his thick iron-gray hair was neatly combed. He declined the cocktails, but drank a small glass of whiskey, straight. And then after a while we had dinner. It was all very pleasant and homey, and I was glad I had come.

After dinner some more people came. The first was Jesse Fortune, Eileen's widowed father, a heavy, red-faced jovial man in corduroy trousers and a flannel shirt, the pockets of which bulged with note books and yellow lead-pencils. With him was a tall, muscular young fellow with thinning yellow hair, a high forehead and rimless glasses. In contrast to Fortune, he was neatly dressed in a double-breasted blue suit, a pale blue shirt and a dark blue knit tie His name was Carl Sarken and he seemed a little ill at ease. Jesse Fortune's loud laugh boomed through the house as he joked with Homer Hollis.

Under cover of the general conversation, I said to Sandy: "I gather that Corduroy Pants is Eileen's old man, but what about the other guy? Relation?"

"No," she said. "To tell you the truth, I'm rather surprised that he's here. A kind of a delicate situation. You see, he was in love with Eileen, too—still is, I suppose. And then Ralph and Eileen became engaged, just before he enlisted."

"What's so delicate about that?" I asked. "The best man won."

"Well, maybe you're right, but Ralph and Earl used to be good friends. They grew up together, and they both went to Ohio State to major in agriculture. Jesse Fortune buys cattle for Earl—I suppose he talked him into coming along."

"He seems like a nice enough guy," I said, and I turned my attention to Homer Hollis. He told me all about his Hereford bull which had won a ribbon at the county fair that fall, and then our talk turned to hunting. He said there were lots of birds, and that he had left some corn shocks and brush standing to provide cover for them. He also told me that the morning hunting party would consist of himself, Sandy, Ralph, Eileen Fortune, Jesse Fortune and myself.

"Aren't you going to invite young Sarken?" I asked.

He puffed on his pipe, said: "That's up to Ralph."

I heard the rattle of gravel as a car came up the drive. Sandy got up and went to the door, and in a minute she came back with a pretty dark-haired girl. The girl was dressed in a fleece-lined jacket, gray flannel slacks and a tight-fitting green sweater. She looked over the room and flung her long black hair back from her cold-flushed face.

"I heard that Ralph was home, and I just wanted to say 'hello' for old time's sake. But I didn't know it was a party."

Ralph Hollis lifted his long frame from his chair, crossed the room and took her hand in both of his. "How are you, Judy?" he said in his easy, friendly way. "Will you have a drink? We have Manhattans—in honor of Mr. Bennett, there—and plain whiskey."

She looked at me, and for a second her gray eyes grew cold and appraising. I pulled myself out of my chair, and Ralph said: "Judy Kirkland—Jim Bennett, the famous private detective. But don't get any ideas, Jim. She hates men. She devotes her life to her dogs and horses."

Judy Kirkland said: "How amusing. Like Perry Mason?"

"No," I said. "Like Fearless Fosdick."

She laughed, and held out her hand. It was cool and soft. She had a clear, faintly tanned complexion, a straight nose, sharply defined cheek-bones, a wide, brightly-painted mouth. "Just kidding, Mr. Bennett. I've heard of you, of course. Don't pay any attention to Ralph. And if Manhattans are good enough for you, they're swell with me."

She nodded at the rest, and I saw her eyes narrow very slightly when she saw Eileen Fortune. I led her to the table and poured a drink. Sandy Hollis said: "Don't forget, Judy. I'm the gal what brung him."

Judy Kirkland laughed again, slid the big soft coat from her shoulders, took the glass from my hand, grasped my arm and led me to the fire. I pulled up a chair for her, and we both sat down. She turned and said to Ralph Hollis: "Come over, Ralph, and tell me all about the war."

Out of the corner of my eye I saw Eileen Fortune's chin tremble very slightly, and there was a swift expression of dismay—maybe fear—on her face. Then she dropped her eyes and sat with her hands in her lap.

"Not much to tell, Judy," Ralph said. "Anything special you want to know about?"

"Yes," Judy Kirkland said. "There is. How did you like the Japanese girls?"

Eileen Fortune got to her feet, and she stood trembling for a second, her small fists clenched. She opened her mouth as though to speak. But she didn't say anything. She turned and walked swiftly out of the room.

I expected Ralph Hollis to get up and follow her. But I was wrong. It was Earl Sarken.

FOR HALF a minute there was silence in the room. And then Sandy got up and turned on the radio. After that, everyone began to talk at once. All except Ralph Hollis. He just sat slumped in his chair and looked at his fingernails. Judy Kirkland glanced at me, a bright wicked gleam in her gray eyes.

"Did I say something?" she asked.

"Apparently," I said.

"Oh, nuts," she said. "She shouldn't be so touchy." She stared moodily into the fire and gave me a ringside view of her profile.

Homer Hollis stood up and yawned. He took out a gold watch and began to wind it. "Well, guess I'll turn in. If I'm going hunting in the morning, I got to get up early and get the chores out of the way."

"I'll help, Dad," Ralph Hollis said.

"No, son," he said, smiling in his gentle way. "You stay in bed. You got to take it easy for a while and get some meat back on your bones."

Ralph grinned up at him. "Don't baby me, Dad."

His father nodded to the room in general, and he and Mrs. Hollis left the room. Judy Kirkland told me about her pair of Irish setters, and Jesse Fortune moved over to Ralph Hollis, got out a note book and one of his many yellow pencils and discussed the cattle market in loud tones. And then presently we heard the grind of an automobile starter outside, and then the lights of a car headed down the drive towards the highway.

Judy Kirkland said over her shoulder: "Ralph, Earl's a fine pal of yours. He's taking your gal home."

Ralph shrugged his wide shoulders and got to his feet. "Yeah, looks like it," he said, carelessly. He finished his drink in one swallow. "Good night, everyone," he said, and left the room.

Judy Kirkland said bitterly: "Eileen doesn't know what she's got."

Jesse Fortune looked at her quickly, and Sandy said: "Yes, Ralph's as good as they come—even if he is my brother."

Judy Kirkland finished her drink, stood up, and placed the glass on the mantel. "Have to be going," she said. "Nice to have met you, Mr. Bennett. Will you be staying here long?"

"Until Sunday," I said.

"Maybe I'll see you around," she said, and she picked up her coat.

"Join us tomorrow," Sandy said.

"Thanks, Sandy, but I'd better not." She went out.

Through the window I saw the lights of her car turn into the main highway and head north, fast. I remembered that Earl Sarken and Eileen Fortune had headed north, too.

In the morning everything was all right—at least, on the surface. Jesse Fortune and his daughter arrived right after breakfast, and Eileen and Ralph were friendly and casual, and they even held hands beneath the table while we all had an extra cup of coffee. Homer Hollis handed me a .16 gauge double-barreled shotgun and a handful of shells, and we all went outside.

It was a fine day—cold, but with a bright sun shining over the brown fields. In the woods the remnants of autumn leaves clung to almost bare branches. The six of us walked across a big field filled with corn stalk stubble and drying shocks, and my gun made a pleasant weight in the crook of my arm. We were spread out about ten yards apart, with Homer Hollis on my left, and Jesse Fortune on my right. Sandy and Ralph were on the wings, and Eileen Fortune moved across the field between her father and Ralph Hollis.

Off to my right a pheasant left the shelter of a corn shock and shot into the air. The sun glinted on the bright red and green and gold of its feathers. Homer Hollis shouted: "Sandy! Take it!"

I watched Sandy whip her trim little .12 gauge to her shoulder, saw the gleaming blue barrel follow the flight of the bird, heard the clean crack of her shot.

The bird dropped. Sandy ran to pick it up and held it proudly aloft for us to see. We all gathered around to admire her kill, and Jesse Fortune's laugh boomed out.

"First blood," he said. "We'll have to do something about that. Can't let the women get ahead of us, can we, Homer? You and I will take a stroll over to my place to a thicket I've been watching."

Our party split up. It suited me, because I figured that six in a bunch was too many, even if we were spread out. Homer Hollis, Jesse Fortune and Eileen Fortune struck out across the field towards the Fortune boundary line, and Sandy, Ralph Hollis and I headed in the opposite direction.

We didn't see any birds. When we reached the edge of a deep ravine we heard the sound of gunfire, and when I looked questioningly at Sandy, she furrowed her pretty brows in a frown. Another shot rang out in the cold November air. It came from a valley over the crest of the ravine.

"Is that your Dad and the Fortunes?" I asked Ralph.

"No. I don't think so. Probably some of those damned city hunters on the place without permission. Every year out-of-town hunters flood this whole section. Folks here in the county have to post 'No Hunting' signs in self protection, but it doesn't do much good. Dad never minded a fellow hunting on his place—if he asked permission. Come on."

He went down into the ravine and started up the other side. Sandy and I followed him. A gun cracked again, and something struck my hat brim, like a pebble falling, and the dry branches of the trees around us rattled faintly. Ahead of us, Ralph gained the top of the opposite side of the ravine, and for an instant his tall frame was silhouetted against the bright blue sky. In that instant the unseen gun spoke again—twice—and I saw a pheasant rise over the crest of the hill. I raised my gun, but Sandy's stricken voice stopped me.

"Jim! Ralph's hurt!"

I looked upwards, and I saw Ralph Hollis slump and stagger forward. He dropped his gun and hung limply against the trunk of a big beech tree. And then he slowly slid to the ground.

I reached him first. There was no blood yet, but I could see where the bird shot had entered. Narrow black furrows slanted over and across his right shoulder and chest, leaving ragged tears in his leather jacket. He stretched forward on the ground and laid his cheek against the dry brown leaves. He began to cough, and the leaves were suddenly stained red.

CHAPTER TWO
TARGET PRACTICE

AS I kneeled beside him, I snapped at Sandy: Run to the house and call a doctor. I'll bring him in."

For an instant she stood still looking down at her brother, her face drained white. And then she turned and ran like a young deer, down the ravine, her reddish hair glinting in the sunlight.

I turned Ralph Hollis on his back, and I un-zipped his leather jacket. The shotgun pellets had penetrated deeply, and blood was already soaking his flannel shirt.

I said: "Ralph—how are you?"

He tried to grin, but caught his lip with his teeth in pain. "Hurts—like—hell." He started to cough.

I leaned low and gathered his long body into my arms. As I started to rise, I heard a sound below me. Judy Kirkland was coming up the hill directly beneath us. She was dressed in the same fleece-lined short coat, but had changed her slacks for trim-fitting gabardine breeches and high laced boots. Her generous mouth looked redder than ever beneath big dark sun glasses. Over her long black hair she wore a long-billed red cap, like a baseball player's. She reached the top of the ravine, panting, as I stood erect with Ralph Hollis in my arms. His eyes were closed now.

"Were you doing that shooting?" I asked.

She looked at the limp form of Ralph, and her face went white. "Yes—I—I guess so. I was standing down there in the thicket—I saw a bird come up out of this ravine—did I—"

"Yes," I said, turning away with my burden. "You hit Ralph." I started down the ravine, trying to hold the wounded man as gently as possible.

She scrambled after me. "Wait," she said. "I—"

"Wait, hell," I snapped over my shoulder. "This boy has got to get to a doctor. Bring the guns."

She gathered up the two shotguns, and I could hear her following me, slipping and sliding on the hill.

I figured Ralph Hollis weighed about a hundred and sixty. I tip the scales at one-ninety, and before I reached the farmhouse I was afraid my arms were going to drop off. But I made it, with Judy Kirkland right behind me. I carried Ralph Hollis into the kitchen and through the house to the long living room. I laid him down on a divan before the fireplace. Mrs. Hollis followed me in from the kitchen, wringing her hands.

Sandy appeared. "Dr. Payne is on his way over," she said.

I unbuttoned Ralph Hollis' shirt. There was a lot of blood now, but I couldn't tell how badly he was hit. There were a couple of pellets clinging to his undershirt, and I thought that was a good sign—the shotgun charge had apparently been nearly spent before it struck him. And then I remembered the blood on the leaves, and I knew that at least one of the slugs had gone deep.

Ralph Hollis opened his eyes and smiled faintly. "Worse—than Iwo," he said.

From behind me, Judy Kirkland said: "These damn glasses—I'm supposed to wear them in the sun—I—I didn't see Ralph. All I saw was the bird rising—" Her voice choked off.

A car came up the drive fast, and Sandy said: "That's the doctor." She ran to the door.

The doctor was a tall young man, hatless, wearing a blue wool muffler and a gray tweed overcoat. He had short, curly black hair, and a lean, dark, Indian-like face. He knelt beside Ralph, and from a bag he took a pair of small, blunt-edged scissors. Skillfully he cut away the blood-soaked undershirt. His hands were big and clean, strong-looking. He took one look, and got to his feet.

"We'll have to get him to the hospital. A couple of those slugs are pretty deep—might be in the lung. I'll take him in my car."

"He coughed some blood, Doc," I said. "Right after he was hit."

He gave me a quick look, as though he noticed me for the first time. Then he nodded, and grasped Ralph Hollis behind the shoulders. "You help," he said to me.

I grabbed the wounded man's feet and the two of us gently carried him out to the doctor's sedan. We laid him on the back seat, and Sandy handed me a blanket to wrap him in. I got in beside him and held an arm beneath his shoulders. The doctor climbed behind the wheel.

Sandy said: "Do you need me, Doctor?" He shook his head, stepped on the starter. And then Judy Kirkland opened the car door and got in beside him. "No," he snapped. "You stay here."

She got out again, a dazed expression on her face. I felt the car's rear wheels skid on the gravel, and we took off. I looked out the rear window, and I saw Sandy, Mrs. Hollis and Judy Kirkland stand in the drive. We swung into the highway and headed for town. I heard the doctor muttering to himself, and I said: "What?"

"No sense in taking her along," he said over his shoulder. "Judy, I mean. She's caused enough trouble already. She's always causing trouble. Last week one of her damned dogs bit a patient of mine, and the week before that she smacked her car into one of Ed Hogan's sows and killed her dead. She's a menace to the community."

Ralph Hollis began to groan, and I felt the speed of the car increase. In five minutes we were in town and turning into a cement drive in front of the hospital. The doctor stopped his car at a rear entrance in front of a wide door. We carried Ralph Hollis inside. Orderlies came up then with a wheeled stretcher. The doctor barked quick orders, and then I found myself in an elevator moving slowly upwards.

"Surgery," the doctor said, and the elevator stopped. I helped to wheel Ralph Hollis out into a corridor. The doctor said: "Thanks. What's your name?"

"Bennett—Jim Bennett."

"Stick around, Jim. I'll run you back to the Hollis place."

"O.K., Doc," I said, and I watched them wheel Ralph Hollis into a room at the far end of the corridor. Dr. Payne entered a door at the side. I timed him. In exactly three minutes he came out dressed in what looked like white pajamas and a white skull cap.

"A hell of a note," he said to me as he passed. "Three women ready to pop babies any minute, and an office full of patients," and he disappeared into the operating room.

I sat down on a bench and looked at old copies of magazines. In fifteen minutes the surgery door swung open and I got a whiff of ether. Two nurses wheeled Ralph Hollis to the elevator. He lay very still, swathed in white, his face greasy and composed. Dr. Payne came out and went into the dressing room again. He emerged—five minutes, this time—and said to me: "Let's go."

"Think he'll be all right," he said, as we descended in the elevator. "Two slugs just penetrated the lung wall. Pretty lucky. Nasty, though. How did it happen?"

We drove back towards the Hollis farm, and I told him all I knew about the accident. As we started to climb the hill out of the valley, I said: "You can drop me at the curve above the Hollis place."

Dr. Payne swung his bright black eyes on me for an instant, and then he looked back at the road ahead. "Bennett," he said, casually, "I've heard of you. Police Department, F.B.I.—"

"Relax," I said. "I'm just a private dick. Sandy Hollis works for me, and I'm down here for a little pheasant shooting."

He lifted one hand from the wheel and snapped his fingers. "I knew it. Something to do with the law. I'll let you out at the curve, but it won't do any good. Judy Kirkland is a hellion, and Ralph Hollis jilted her for Eileen Fortune just before he went in the army, but Judy wouldn't try to kill him for that. She isn't that screwy."

I laughed. "Doc, you've got a good imagination. I want to walk from the curve because I need the exercise."

"Sure, sure," he said. "And look over the scene of the crime—isn't that what you call it?—on the way." He braked his car and pulled to the side of the road. "Well, here's the curve. How long are you going to be around here?"

"Until Sunday."

"Good. How about stopping in tonight—after office hours? I've got some Scotch I've been hoarding."

"Sounds good," I said. "Can I bring Sandy?"

"Sure. I ought to be through by ten-thirty. Sandy knows where I live."

I got out and stood in the road. "Thanks for the lift. Do you think Ralph will be O.K.?"

"I think so—if nothing turns up. I'll check him in a couple of hours."

HE WAVED a hand, jockeyed his car around in the road, and headed back towards town. I watched his blue sedan until it was out of sight, and then I climbed the fence and struck out across the fields. The hands on my wrist watch stood at a quarter of twelve. I figured that Ralph had been shot at about ten-thirty in the morning.

I went through a thick woods and emerged on the crest of the ravine above the beech tree, imagining that I was Ralph, and then three minutes along the ridge and I came to the tree, and then I stood and looked down into the shallow valley below. I saw the stretch of thicket out of which Judy Kirkland had emerged, and where she said she had been standing when she fired at the pheasant rising from the ravine behind Ralph Hollis. I shifted my position a little until I thought I was standing in exactly the same spot in which I had seen Ralph just before the shotgun charge had smacked him. I stood beside the tree, imagining that I was Ralph, and that Judy Kirkland was standing in the thicket directly below me with her gun poised for a shot at a bird rising directly behind me. I put myself in Judy's place, standing in thick underbrush, wearing dark sun glasses, and drawing a bead on a bird shooting fast into the sky.

Then I leaned against the tree, and I said to myself: *Bennett, you're a suspicious so-and-so. This shooting is an accident, pure and simple....*

And then a gun cracked nearby. Splinters of bark sprayed out from the tree close beside my head. I slammed myself to the ground, automatically reached for the .38 beneath my left arm. But it wasn't there, of course. It was in my bag in my room at the Hollis farmhouse. I just hugged the dry leaves and waited.

The woods were silent. I couldn't hear anything but the chirping of sparrows in the tree above me. And then a cock-bird called from the thicket below me, and I saw a brown, drab-colored hen rise from the field on my left and fly towards the thicket. And then there was more silence. I thought of Daniel Boone and Davey Crockett, and I wondered what they would have done in the same situation, with redskins skulking out there in the woods, maybe drunk on fire-water and itching for my scalp. I figured they would do the same thing I was doing—lay low.

I waited maybe five minutes before I began to crawl backwards on my stomach. My coat got bunched up around my neck, and my clothes got covered with burrs and dirt, but I finally made it to the bottom of the ravine. Then I got cautiously to my feet and looked up at the exposed ridge of the ravine I had just left. I figured that the shot had come from a field on my left, and I remembered that an old-fashioned rail fence had zigzagged along its boundary. I walked along the bottom of the ravine, and when I came to the end of it I climbed slowly to the top and looked over. The rail fence was close—maybe fifty feet away—and I looked long and carefully. But I didn't see a thing. Nothing but brown fields and woods and the highway.

Whoever had taken a shot at me—if someone had intentionally taken a shot—had cleared out. I walked across the fields and back to the farmhouse. On the way I wondered if people in this part of the country hunted pheasants with rifles, and I decided that they didn't.

As I turned the corner of the barn, I saw Homer Hollis standing on the back porch filling his pipe.

"Hi, Homer," I said.

"Hello, Jim." He looked down at me from over his lighted match. I sat on the steps and lit a cigarette. He sat down beside me and thoughtfully puffed his pipe.

"Mom and Sandy have gone into the hospital," he said.

"Doc said he thought Ralph would be all right. Close shave, though," I said. "Did you just get in?"

"A spell back—right after you took Ralph to town, Mom rang the dinner bell and called us in. Eileen went straight to the hospital. I want to thank you for carrying our boy all that way."

"Forget it," I said. "Did Jesse Fortune go home?"

"Yes—right after we split up. Said he had forgotten about a cattle buyer from Cleveland he was to meet at his place. He said he'd come back, but I guess he got tied up with that fellow."

There was silence on the steps for a minute. The smoke from Homer's pipe curled up into the cold November sunlight. He shifted his position and cleared his throat.

"Jim—what do you make of this?" he asked, his eyes on the distant fields.

I looked quickly at him. "How do you mean?" I asked.

"About Ralph. Do you think it was an accident?"

I shrugged. "Sure. They happen all the time. Why?"

He gave me a shy, sidelong look, and struck another match and held it to his pipe. "I'm probably a suspicious old coot," he said, "but I can't help but remember that Judy Kirkland was awful sweet on Ralph—still is, for all I know. She and Ralph had some kind of quarrel just before he went away. And then the first thing I knew he was engaged to marry Eileen Fortune. That's the way things stood when he left."

"Do you think Judy shot him deliberately—because she was jealous?" I asked.

Homer Hollis made a quick motion with his hand. "Now, now, I don't know. I just wondered—this is just between you and me. I thought, you being a big city detective, and all..."

I smiled grimly to myself. I still remembered the wicked smack of that bullet as it hit the tree beside my head.

"What about Carl Sarken?" I asked. "The fellow who left with Eileen last night?"

"He's in love with her," Homer said. "Has been for a long time—long before Ralph went away, while Ralph and Judy was still going together. He was turned down in the draft—sinus trouble—and after Ralph went away he tried to make hay with Eileen again."

"Did he get any place?" I asked.

It was Homer Hollis' turn to shrug. "How can you tell? I know that her father was in favor of it. Jesse Fortune is in a bad way. This summer he lost all he had—and more too, I hear—in a stock gamble. The whole county knows about it. And Earl Sarken is well fixed. His folks owned half of this county before they died. Earl got it all. I figured that Jesse Fortune could use a son-in-law like Earl. But as for how Eileen feels about Earl—I don't know. She could have had him, but she picked Ralph."

"What does Sarken do?" I asked.

"He doesn't do much of anything. Lives in town, has a man running his farms, and what he calls a 'foreman' on each farm—like a factory. He learned his farming in college—but he makes it pay."

My mind began to click in the old familiar routine. "Would Eileen marry Sarken—if it wasn't for Ralph?" I asked.

His eyes shifted a little, and he knocked the ashes out of his pipe against the side of the steps.

"Maybe," he said, "Second choice. But not while Ralph was alive."

I sighed, and flicked my cigarette against the wall of a chicken coop. A hell of a vacation I was getting. The same old routine, complete with attempted murder and assorted suspects. It didn't make any difference—roaring, noisy city, or quiet, peaceful countryside—human emotions and desires went on just the same. I was stuck, and I couldn't help it, and so I forgot about pheasant hunting and chicken dinners and wood fires in a farmhouse living room, and I figured I might as well go whole hog.

A CAR came up the drive and stopped beside the porch. It was Judy Kirkland's red convertible. As I opened the door for her, I saw a rifle leaning against the seat.

It was a .30 caliber Winchester carbine.

Judy Kirkland said: "Mr. Bennett, I feel like crying for joy. I just came from the hospital, and they told me that Ralph would be all right."

I nodded and picked up the rifle. "Nice gun," I said, and I opened the breech. The chamber was empty of slugs. I leaned it back against the seat.

She was watching me. "I've been shooting rats," she said. "This morning when I opened the corn crib door the floor was moving with them. But I'm rid of them for a while."

"Pretty heavy gun for rats," I said, casually. "Did you shoot them all?"

She laughed. "Oh, no. I caught one of them alive in a trap, and I tarred and feathered it and let it go. It ran straight under the barn and in about one second I heard a tremendous squealing and hundreds of rats poured out of their holes and ran off, the tarred rat trying to keep up with them. The faster he ran, the faster the rest tried to get away from him. It was comical. They won't come back for a long time."

"You're the first girl I ever saw that would think tarring and feathering a rat was comical," I said. "But go on." I grinned at her.

"That's all. It's an old Ohio trick—honest. For some reason, they're deathly afraid of tar and feathers—maybe they think it's a ferret. I don't know. Anyhow, it works."

She got out of the car, spoke to Homer Hollis, and sat down on the steps. She took a crumpled pack of cigarettes from her jacket pocket, lit one, and inhaled deeply. "I still don't see how I could have hit him," she said. "But the sun, and those damned glasses—"

Homer Hollis didn't say anything.

A car came up the drive then, stopped behind Judy's convertible, and Sandy, Mrs. Hollis and Eileen Fortune got out. "Jesse had to go to Cleveland with that cattle buyer," Sandy said, "and Eileen is staying with us until tomorrow."

We all went in and had lunch, only Mrs. Hollis called it "dinner." Judy Kirkland stayed. Afterwards, Homer announced that he was going to town. He invited me to go along, but I told him that I'd like to try again for a pheasant. "Try the bottom land below the south pasture," he advised.

I followed him outside, and Sandy gave me a questioning look as I passed her. But I didn't invite her to accompany me.

Outside, I said to Homer: "Do you really think she might have meant to kill him and make it appear like an accident?"

His lean face was grim. "I know this—Judy Kirkland is a wildcat when she's crossed. Her dad was the same way. Orville Kirkland had the meanest temper in this county. I saw him kill a horse once—with a singletree. It was a good horse, too—just balky because a stallion was in the next stall. Orville was sorry afterwards just like Judy is probably sorry now."

"I see," I said. "What kind of a guy is this Dr. Payne?"

He gave me a quick look. "Doc Payne? He's as good as they come. Been here about three years. Hung out his shingle right after Ralph went away. After old Doc Gilmore died, we called Payne when we wanted a doctor—like when Mom had the flu last winter, and when I sprained my ankle digging post holes. Doc Payne's all right."

"Married?" I asked.

"No. I guess he's too busy to get married, but I hear half the girls in the county are making eyes at him."

Homer climbed into a small truck, lit his pipe, and said: "If you need any more shells, they're on the top shelf in the pantry."

After he had driven away I went into the barn and hunted around until I found a sharp wood chisel and a hammer. I put them in a pocket of my hunting coat, picked up the shotgun, and walked down to the end of the back lane. I climbed a fence and headed across the fields towards the ravine where Ralph Hollis had been shot. This time I approached from the north, and I walked in the bottom of the ravine until I reached the big beech tree. I laid the shotgun on a log and made sure this time that my .38 was in my pocket, loose and handy. The familiar smooth feel of it made me happier, and I slowly ascended the steep side of the ravine to the crest. When I neared the top, I flopped on my belly, like an advanced scout for a wagon train, and looked over the countryside. I couldn't see a thing except an occasional car droning along the distant highway.

I got to my feet and went to work on the tree with my hammer and chisel. The slug was buried deep, but I finally got it out and examined it. It was flattened and out of shape, but I knew that it was a .30 caliber rifle bullet.

I put the shapeless piece of lead in a pocket of my flannel shirt, and I buttoned the flap. And then I heard a slight sound behind me, like the snapping of a twig.

I whirled, my hand gripping the gun in my pocket.

I DON'T know where he came from, but Earl Sarken was standing there, ten feet away, watching me. He was dressed in the fanciest hunting outfit this side of Fifth Avenue. Bright red wool hunting coat, thirty-dollar whipcord breeches, polished brown boots, a corduroy peaked cap, dark sun glasses. He was carrying a beautiful handmade sixteen-gauge shotgun with ventilated sights and ornamental scroll work in silver on the stock.

"Mr. Bennett, I believe," he said, bowing slightly. I saw then that he was drunk and swaying very slightly on his feet.

"Hello, Sarken," I said. "I didn't hear you come up."

"That's not surprising," he said. "You were making a lot of noise."

I admitted ruefully to myself that he was right.

"A lot of noise, Mr. Bennett," he repeated. "You'll scare all the birds away."

"Sorry," I said. "I guess I thought I was the only one hunting on Homer's place this afternoon."

"What are you hunting, Mr. Bennett? Mushrooms? I don't seem to see your gun."

I nodded towards the bottom of the ravine where my shotgun leaned against the log. Sarken pushed his dark glasses up on his high forehead and peered down into the ravine. "Ah, yes," he said. "I see it now."

He took off his glasses, put them in a breast pocket of his red coat, transferred his gun to the crook of his left arm, fumbled inside his coat, and took out an over-sized silver flask. He unscrewed the cap, let it dangle to the neck of the flask by a silver chain, and held it out to me. "Have a drink," he said.

I took the flask and tilted it to my mouth. It was good brandy, smooth and hot. "Thanks," I said, handing it back to him.

He took a long swallow, replaced the cap, and put the flask on the ground at his feet. "Help yourself when you're ready," he said. He lit a cigarette and squinted at me. "Look," he said abruptly, "Homer don't care if I hunt on his place. Homer always says: 'Earl, anytime you want to hunt on my place, you go right ahead.' Homer is a good guy, but I haven't got any use for his son. We used to be pals—roomed together at Columbus—but is it my fault I didn't get in the army and be a hero? Ralph had a girl—why in hell does he want to take mine, too? I think Ralph Hollis is a lousy double-crosser." He stopped talking, and his lower lip stuck out, like a pouting child's. He stooped down, picked up the flask, offered it to me.

"No, thanks," I said. "Did you know that Ralph Hollis is in the hospital? Judy Kirkland shot him this morning."

He looked at me, his mouth open. "Judy—shot him? Is he—"

"Don't get your hopes up," I said. "He isn't dead. It was an accident. Happened right here, while they were hunting. Judy shot at a bird with the sun in her eyes—"

"Accident, hell," he sneered. "Judy Kirkland had a right to shoot him. I don't blame her."

"Attempted murder, would you say?" I asked softly.

He passed a hand over his eyes. "No—no—I didn't mean that—"

"By the way," I said, "were you hunting around here this morning, along about ten-thirty?"

He looked at me steadily for a couple of seconds. Then he laughed shortly. "I forgot—you're a big shot detective. Got to run down clues, and all that. No, Mr. Bennett, I wasn't hunting around here this morning." He said the last in falsetto, mocking tones.

Earl Sarken was getting on my nerves. I started down the ravine to pick up my shotgun. I had the bullet out of the tree, and I wanted to get going.

"Hey," Sarken said. "Wait, you. I'm not through talking to you."

"Sorry," I said over my shoulder. "I gotta go."

Behind me, Sarken's voice was suddenly rasping. "Dammit, I said wait."

I turned slowly, looked up at him, and I stared straight down the twin blue barrels of his fancy shotgun. He stood swaying slightly, his feet apart, and I could see that his finger was tight on the triggers.

I was still holding the hammer in my hand. I started back up to the ridge of the ravine, and I grinned at Sarken. He was drunk, and I didn't know what he had in mind. I had to play it careful.

"Now, is that nice?" I asked as I gained the ridge. "Put that gun down and let's have a drink. O.K.?"

He backed up slightly, and swung the double barrels toward me. I stood still, grinning at him.

"Take it easy, bud," I said. "That blunderbuss might go off."

"I want to know why you're snooping around here," he said stubbornly. He kept the gun leveled at my chest.

I was through monkeying with him. "Now, look, sonny," I said, and as I spoke I swung the hammer in my right hand against the barrel of his gun. He stumbled backwards and pulled both triggers, and I heard the shot blasting into the bare branches of the trees on the side of the ravine. I bored right on in, and I got Sarken by the front of his thick red coat. I pulled him in close to me and I slapped him hard across the mouth. His knees caved in, and he went down. I jerked him to his feet, slapped him again, and shoved him away from me. He sprawled on his back in the dead leaves, and his legs moved a little.

I picked up his shotgun and noted the dent my hammer had made in the barrel. I broke the gun, ejected the two empty shells. Then I leaned over Sarken and took six extra shells from his coat pocket.

I said: "Get up, and get going. I'm just a city punk, but I know enough not to carry both a loaded gun and a bottle into the woods."

He got slowly to his feet and sullenly brushed off his fancy clothes. He kept his head down. I handed him the gun. "I'll keep the shells. And I want to talk to you about a couple of things—when you're sober."

He took his gun, and without a word he turned and walked slowly along the ridge of the ravine. I watched him until he was out of sight, and then I got my gun and walked back to the Hollis farm house. It was only three o'clock in the afternoon, but I wasn't used to the fresh air, I guess, and the outdoor exercise. I went quietly up to my room and took a nap.

CHAPTER THREE
SHOWDOWN

SANDY KNOCKED at my door at five-thirty. "Time to get ready for dinner," she said.

The Hollis farm was not far from town, and they had most of the city folk's conveniences—hot and cold water, gas and electricity, two bathrooms. I took a shower and shaved.

To me, the hour before dinner is the best time of the day—a bath, clean clothes, a drink or two, that pleasant feeling of relaxation. Only my mind didn't relax. As I dressed, I thought about the day's events, and I knew that whatever I did about them would have to be done tonight.

I went downstairs and walked into the living room. A fire was burning in the fireplace, and Sandy had set out a tray containing ice, cherries, vermouth, whiskey, bitters and a stirring pitcher. Eileen Fortune sat in front of the fire. She was the only person in the room, although I could hear Sandy talking to her mother in the kitchen. Eileen looked up and smiled at me as I entered the room.

She nodded at the tray. "Sandy said you could make your own Manhattans tonight," she said.

"Good," I said. "Will you have one?"

"Thank you, I feel as though I need a drink."

I measured, poured, stirred, speared a cherry, handed her a glass, filled one for myself. Then I sat down beside her on the divan in front of the fire. She sipped at her drink, and for the first time I looked at her carefully.

She had long yellow hair, shining and clean, which fell to her shoulders in soft curls. Her small face was delicately made, and her features were good—a slightly tilted nose, a firm, small chin, blue eyes, level brows. She was small, about five foot one or two, and I figured she weighed around one-five, maybe less. She was dressed in a bluish tweed suit, a white blouse, and perky, stubby, high-heeled brown shoes. Eileen Fortune was a girl any man could be proud of, and I didn't blame Earl Sarken for carrying the torch for her. Mentally I gave her credit for competing—and apparently winning—against a wise and slick girl like Judy Kirkland.

"Any luck today?" she asked, and I saw Ralph Hollis' diamond glitter on the third finger of her left hand.

"Not even one bird," I said, stretching out and taking the first sip of my drink. The firelight flickered on the walls, and I suddenly regretted that I couldn't just stay here, talking to a girl like Eileen Fortune and feeling the warmth of the fire on my face.

She said: "Poor Judy. She feels badly about—the accident."

"One of those things," I said drowsily, making conversation.

"I hate Judy Kirkland," she said.

I looked at her. She was staring into the fire, and there were tears in her eyes.

Her remark irritated me. "Why?" I asked. "You've got him, haven't you?"

She looked at the toes of her trim little shoes. "I don't know," she said slowly. "Before he went away, everything was fine. He told me it was all over between him and Judy, and I believed him. For three years I waited for him, and I wrote to him every day. And then he came back, and he didn't act the same. Maybe it was the war. I trust Ralph, but I don't trust her—Judy, I mean. She had him once, and she wants to have him again. Once, while Ralph was away, she told me that if she couldn't have Ralph, I wouldn't have him, either. And she's so smart, and so clever—so much more clever than I am...."

I squirmed on the divan. "Don't worry," I said. "Ralph will be well soon, and then you can get married, and everything will be all right."

I said to myself: *Jim Bennett, private investigations—and advice to the lovelorn,* and I took another swallow of my drink.

"I wish I could believe that," Eileen Fortune said.

"What are you worrying about?" I asked. "If you don't get Ralph, you can always fall back on Earl Sarken." It was a hell of a thing to say to a dewey-eyed bride-to-be, but I wanted to get her reaction.

I was disappointed. She merely looked at me for a startled instant. "You know about Earl?" she asked, wide-eyed. "But, Mr. Bennett, that was over long ago. Earl is nice, and he took me home last night because he felt sorry for me, but Ralph is the man I'm going to marry. Why mention Earl?"

I shrugged. "It's obvious that he's nuts about you."

She sighed, and continued to stare into the fire. "Poor Earl. Maybe I should have married him. Papa likes him, and he is very wealthy. I probably would have married him long ago—if it hadn't been for Ralph."

It was my turn to sigh. Nothing in life ever seemed to fit. Earl Sarken loved Eileen Fortune. But Eileen loved

Ralph Hollis. Judy Kirkland loved Ralph Hollis, too. But who did Ralph Hollis love?

I got up then and made myself another drink.

AFTER DINNER, I drove Sandy, her mother and father, and Eileen Fortune in to the hospital to see Ralph. I let them out, drove down to the middle of Main Street and parked. I went into a place called Dan's Ohio Grill, had a bourbon and soda, and asked the barkeep where Earl Sarken lived.

He shoved a glass towards me, said: "He lives on the north corner of Crawford and Tymocktee, south of the high school, but if you want to see him, he's in the back room playing poker."

"That's service," I said. "Thanks," I finished my drink and walked to an alcove at the rear of the long bar. Beyond a door marked *Gents* was another door, and I opened it and went in.

The room was small and filled with smoke. Eight men sat at a big round green-covered table. They were playing with chips, but there was also a big mound of bills in the center of the table. Sarken sat facing the door, still dressed in his hunting clothes. His big red coat hung on the back of his chair. There was a highball glass in front of him, but he looked sober. When he saw me, he started to rise.

I held up a palm. "Finish the hand," I said. "I'll be at the bar."

His face looked gray under the bright overhanging light. The other seven men in the stud game turned and looked at me. "Hi, boys," I said. "Sorry to interrupt," and I turned and went back to the bar.

I had another bourbon and soda, and I waited three minutes by the clock on the wall back of the bar. Then I went back to the card room. Earl Sarken's chair was empty. His coat was gone, too. The seven men kept on playing, didn't look up at me.

I said: "Where did he go?"

The man nearest the door said, without taking his eyes from the cards on the table in front of him: "To the john, bud. He'll be back."

Another man said, "I'll raise it five," and the chips rattled. The seven kept on playing, ignoring me. I went back out and into the room labeled *Gents.* There were a couple of guys in there, but neither of them were Earl Sarken. I went back to the card room, and I spotted a door beyond the card table. I crossed to the door, and I said: "Thanks, boys. You meant the lady's john, no doubt." I opened the door and I stepped out into a dark alley.

I stood still for a minute, trying to see in the darkness. A cold November wind blew up the alley, and I transferred my .38 from my inside coat pocket to my overcoat pocket, and I turned up my collar. Twenty yards up the alley I heard a slight sound—like metal moving on bricks. I spotted a big ash can then, and I moved slowly towards it, my hand on my gun in my pocket. My heels made a soft clicking noise on the bricks, and from the lighted street beyond came the sound of traffic and an occasional tooting of a horn. The alley was short, but the sounds seemed curiously far away, and I suddenly felt alone and a little scared.

The can moved again, very slightly, with a small scraping sound. I backed up against the wall on my right and I cleared the gun from my pocket.

"All right, Sarken," I said loudly. "Come out of there."

And then the narrow alley roared and shook with gunfire, and bright bursts of flame stabbed out from behind the ash can. I hit the bricks, and I fired back, and heard the returning splatter of slugs on the wall above me. And then a bullet hit the pavement directly in front of my face, and brick dust sprayed up into my eyes. For a couple of seconds I couldn't see, and I fired blindly at the ash can. I heard someone pounding up the alley, and I got one eye open in time to see a dark figure dart out of the end of the alley and disappear.

I stood up and wiped the dust from my eyes and re-filled the cylinder of my .38. I started up the alley towards the street. Someone ran towards me with a flashlight, and put the beam full on my face. I blinked and turned my face away.

"What's going on back here?" a voice asked.

"Take that damn light away," I said.

The light was lowered and I saw the big form of a man. He had a Police Special in his right fist, and the light glittered on a double row of brass buttons.

"Relax, Chief," I said. "I came out of the back door of Dan's and somebody blazed away at me from behind that ash can."

He swung his light at the can. My slugs had torn four big holes in it, and I saw the chipped wall behind it where the other two bullets had struck. I said hastily: "I slung a little lead back at him."

The big cop grunted. "No!" he said with deep sarcasm. "You better come along with me."

The last thing I wanted was to get mixed up with the local law. I was snooping around on something that was none of my business, and I wasn't even hired for the job. If the boss found out about it, he would raise merry hell—not because I was risking my neck, but because I was risking my neck and not getting paid for it.

"Look, Chief," I said, "I'm in kind of a hurry. I can give you all the identification you want. I'm visiting at the Homer Hollis place, and I've got to get back out there."

He just grunted, took me by the arm, and guided me towards the street. I figured that I could make a break, and maybe get away with it, but a gang of nosy onlookers was already peering into the alley and enough commotion had been raised already. I shook off the cop's arm, and walked along at his side.

"We'll just have a little talk with the chief," he said.

"Oh," I said. "I thought you were the chief."

"Shut up," he grunted, and pushed a path for us through the crowd.

At the dinky police station on the ground floor of the city hall there was one man on duty. The chief wasn't there, and they called him at his home. While we waited, the big cop searched me and took my .38.

Chief of Police Wilkens, a skinny, dried-up old codger with a tobacco-stained white mustache, finally came, and I told who I was, and who I worked for. Then I gave him a phony story of trailing a blackmailer from Cleveland, and I gave him an equally phony description of the guy I was supposed to be after. I said I had cornered him in the alley behind Dan's place, but he had gotten away.

It took about a half hour to convince him, but the boss's name carries a lot of weight on almost any police force in the country, and I had the usual identification. The Chief called Homer Hollis at the hospital, and after that it was clear sailing. They gave me back my gun, and I started to leave.

"If you need any help, Mr. Bennett," the chief said, "call on us."

"Thanks, Chief. I'll do that."

I got in my car and went out to the hospital. As soon as I walked inside, I knew that something was wrong. Mrs. Hollis' eyes were red, and Sandy was pale. Eileen Fortune was sobbing openly, and Homer's face was grim.

"Jim, Ralph's worse," he said. "He took a bad turn about an hour ago. Doc Payne is with him now."

I went down the corridor to Ralph's room. The door was closed, and I rapped softly. Dr. Payne poked his dark head out. When he saw me, he crooked a finger, and I tiptoed in. Ralph's long form was beneath a sheet on a narrow hospital bed. His eyes were closed, and he was breathing heavily. His face was flushed with fever.

Dr. Payne whispered: "We're afraid of pneumonia. His temperature started to rise late this afternoon, and I can't get it down."

"We better skip that date for tonight, Doc," I said.

"No, please don't. There is nothing I can do here right now. We're putting on a special nurse, and she'll call me at home if necessary."

"O.K.," I said, and I left.

I drove the rest of them back to the farm. There was a car parked in the drive, and as we stopped a man got out and walked over to us. It was Jesse Fortune.

"I just got in from Cleveland," he said. "I've been waiting here to take Eileen home. Got through with my business sooner than I expected. You ready to go, sis?"

And then he saw the gloomy faces, and Homer Hollis told him about Ralph.

Jesse Fortune ran a big hand over his eyes. "That's too bad. A hell of a note. Homer, is there anything I can do?"

Homer Hollis silently shook his head, and Eileen Fortune ran to her father, buried her face in his coat, and sobbed brokenly. Awkwardly, Jesse Fortune patted his daughter's head. "There, there sis, don't take on. He'll come out of it just fine. You'll see."

Over his daughter's head, he said to Homer: "It's bad for Judy, too. How's she taking it?"

Homer's face was grim. "I wouldn't know, Jesse," he said, shortly, and he went into the house. Mrs. Hollis followed him. Jesse Fortune and his daughter got into their car, and Sandy said to them: "I'll call you, if—"

Fortune said, "We'll appreciate it, Sandy," nodded at me, and drove away.

SANDY AND I stood alone in the driveway. "Sandy," I said, "I've been wanting to talk to you alone all day," and I told her about the rifle slug smacking the tree beside my head, and of my meeting with Earl Sarken, and what had happened behind Dan's Ohio Grill.

When I had finished, she said, "It looks as if you're dragged into a case whether you like it or not."

"Never mind that," I said. "The least I can do is check on it a little—after all, you're the best secretary I ever had. But if I catch you making a report of any of this to the boss—"

She smiled faintly. "Don't worry. But I see no reason why it shouldn't be a regular fee job. Dad is quite bitter about it, and if Ralph's injury wasn't an accident..."

"You can put the police on it," I said.

"Dad wouldn't want that, and I wouldn't, either—at least, not now."

"By the way," I said, "we're calling on Doc Payne to drink a few Scotch highballs. Tell your folks."

She reached up and gently patted my cheek. "You're a pretty nice boss, too," she said, and ran into the house. I turned my car around in the drive, and in a couple of minutes she came out and got in beside me. We drove back into town.

Dr. Payne's house was on a corner at the edge of the business district. A gold and black sign on the front lawn read: *Albert Payne, M.D. Physician and Surgeon.* The lower floor of the house was devoted to his office and waiting room, and he lived in the rooms above.

He was waiting for us, and he already had ice, soda, glasses and a bottle of Scotch on a table. His rooms were comfortable and well furnished, with many books in shelves along the walls. He handed me a tinkling glass, and I stretched out in an over-stuffed chair and lit a cigarette.

"Doc," I said, "you ought to get married. This place is nice, but it needs a woman's touch."

He laughed. "Maybe you're right. Sandy, will you marry me?"

"You'll have to ask my boss," she said.

He grinned at her, and said to me: "Bennett, fire her, will you, and make a lonely man happy?"

"Sorry," I told him. "I've got her under contract."

We talked a while, had some more drinks, and it was all very pleasant. Sandy apparently enjoyed herself, but I knew that she was thinking about Ralph, and several times she asked the doctor about him.

At eleven o'clock the telephone rang. It was on a small stand beside my chair, and I said: "I'll get it."

Sandy's face grew tense, and Dr. Payne started to rise from his chair, but I had the receiver to my ear. "Dr. Payne's residence," I said.

A woman's voice said: "Al?" I knew that voice, and for a split second I hesitated. Then I said, "just a minute," and handed the phone to the doctor.

"Yes," he said, his face very grave. "Oh, yes, Mrs. Cannon. Five minutes apart? Yes... yes... Have Mr. Cannon take you to the hospital. I'll be right out there."

He hung up, and sighed. "I'll have to leave. Mrs. Cannon thinks it's time, but I'll probably be up all night. You folks stay here and enjoy yourselves."

I got to my feet. "No, thanks, Doc. As much as I'd like to be left alone in an apartment with Sandy and a bottle of Scotch, I'm afraid we must leave, too."

We all went downstairs together, and Dr. Payne drove away in his blue sedan. As we got into my car, Sandy said: "Now what?"

"We wait three minutes," I told her, "and then we go to Judy Kirkland's house. Where does she live?"

"I'll show you. She lives alone in a small house here in town. The farm her folks left her is out beyond our place, but she has it rented—she just keeps her dogs and horses there."

We smoked a cigarette, and Sandy said: "Was it Judy who called?"

"Yeah," I said, and I started the motor. "How many guys does she have on the string?"

"You can't tell about Judy," Sandy said.

Judy Kirkland lived in a small frame house on the edge of town. It had been built back from the street, and there was a neat white picket fence surrounding it. I drove slowly past once. Judy's red convertible was parked in a short drive in front of a small garage, but I didn't see any sign of Dr. Payne's car. I turned around and drove back, and then I spotted it. It was parked almost a block away beneath some big oak trees which lined the highway out of town. I stopped a block away in the opposite direction, and I told Sandy to wait for me.

"Can't I go along?" she said.

"No. Your duties with the American Detective Agency are purely secretarial. Sit tight. I'll be back in ten minutes."

She said: "All right, gum-shoe."

I walked back to the corner, and I entered an alley which ran behind the house. There was a light in the kitchen window, and I crossed the back yard and flattened myself against the side of the house. The window was too high for me to look through, and I hunted around for something to stand on. I found a case of empty beer bottles beside the back steps, and I laid the bottles on the grass, one by one. Then I turned the case on end, stood on it, and I had a clear view of the kitchen.

Judy Kirkland and Dr. Payne were seated at a white enameled kitchen table. There was a coffee pot and cups between them, and they were leaning towards each other, talking intently. I could hear the low murmur of their voices, but I couldn't make out the words. I waited and listened, and the minutes ticked by.

Suddenly, Dr. Payne got to his feet, and he pointed a long forefinger at the girl. He talked loud, and I could hear him plainly through the glass.

"You can either stop this nonsense and do as I say," he said, "or you can go to hell. I'm tired of your screwball whims and your crack-pot movie star notions. If you want to marry me, all right. If you don't, say so, and we'll call it quits."

Judy Kirkland's red mouth began to tremble. I had to press my ear against the window to catch her words. "Al, don't talk like that," she said. "You know I love you. Just give me a little time—I've got to get myself straightened out."

"A little time, hell," Dr. Payne shouted. "I've given you all the time I'm going to give you. Make up your mind. After

Ralph Hollis dies, it'll be too late. Make your choice now, and stick by it."

"What about Ralph?" she asked.

"I don't know," he snapped. "That doesn't make any difference. Make up your mind now. Tomorrow will be too late. It's either Ralph Hollis or me, and I want to know which—now!"

She got up from the table and stood in front of him, her arms at her side. He grasped her roughly by the shoulders and pulled her to him. His dark head bent down, and I saw her red-tipped fingers curling around his neck.

I got softly down from the beer case, and went back to the car.

Sandy Hollis said: "Well, Hawkshaw, what did you find out?"

"I don't know," I said, as we drove away. "I don't know."

WE DROVE out to the hospital, and Sandy and I went in and talked to the special nurse on duty in care of Ralph Hollis. She said his condition hadn't changed, that his temperature was the same.

"Naturally, Miss Nusbaum," I said, "we want Mr. Hollis to have every care. From your experience, would you say that Dr. Payne is doing everything possible?"

Sandy gave me a queer look, but I went on: "You understand, Miss Nusbaum, that we have every faith in Dr. Payne, but we just want to be certain that nothing is overlooked which might improve Mr. Hollis' chances for recovery."

The nurse nodded her head vigorously. "Oh, yes. Dr. Payne is very competent. His treatment for Mr. Hollis is standard medical practice for this type of case. Penicillin, drainage—"

"Thank you, Miss Nusbaum," I said, and I took Sandy's arm and led her down the corridor to the hospital office. The nurse on duty there was a beefy matron with a bulldog face and black-ribboned pince-nez.

"Good evening, madam," I said. "I am an attorney representing the family of Mr. Ralph Hollis. Would you, in your great experience, say that his special nurse is competent and trustworthy?"

She looked at me over her glasses and tapped her desk with a lead pencil. "Miss Nusbaum has been with this hospital for years, and I will have you know that she is one of our most experienced and skillful nurses."

"Thank you, madam," I said, quickly, and I led Sandy away.

As we drove away from the hospital, Sandy asked: "Do you think that Dr. Payne—?"

"I stopped thinking two hours ago," I told her. "Direct me to Eileen Fortune's home."

"I don't get it," Sandy said. "Turn right at the next corner. Eileen lives three miles out on the state highway, a mile this side of our place—a big white house on a hill."

When we neared the Fortune farm, I slowed down and looked the place over. The house was dark, but there was a car parked in the drive leading to the barnyard in the rear. My headlights picked up its red tail-lights as we moved slowly past. I looked at the clock on my dash board. Ten minutes of twelve.

"Is that Jesse Fortune's car?" I asked Sandy.

She peered out of the window. "Yes, I think so."

"Look like everybody's in bed to you?"

"Sure does."

"O.K.," I said. "Time's a-wastin'. I'll take you home now."

"Not now, you won't. I'm going with you."

"All right," I said. "But remember—no overtime pay."

"I'll go to the union." She laughed.

I turned on the radio, and we picked up some smooth dance music from Cleveland. "There's a bottle in the glove compartment," I said to Sandy.

She opened the door of the compartment and took out a pint bottle of bourbon. She unscrewed the cap, and tilted the bottle to her lips.

"Ugh," she said in a strangled voice. "You don't happen to have a cold bottle of soda, do you?"

"Sissy," I said, taking the bottle. I suddenly realized that I was tired. It had been a long day, and I wasn't used to tramping the woods on a cold November day. The whiskey tasted good, and perked me up a little. I handed the bottle back to Sandy.

"No, thanks." She shuddered. She replaced the bottle in the dash compartment.

I drove slowly back to town. It was pleasant driving along, listening to the music.

Sandy said: "Jim?"

"Yes, sweetheart."

"Where are we going?"

"To Judy Kirkland's house."

"Why? Again?"

"I want to get my hands on that Winchester carbine of hers."

"To check it with that bullet you dug out of the tree?"

I nodded.

Sandy sighed, but she didn't say anything. When we got into town, the main street was dark and empty, and only an occasional dim street-light glowed yellowly along the short thoroughfare. I parked in the same spot I had before, a block away from Judy Kirkland's house.

"Do you think she'll be in bed?" I asked Sandy.

She shrugged. "Probably."

I got out of the car, and then I thought of something. "You got any idea where she keeps her guns?"

"It might be out at the farm," Sandy said. "But if she brought it in with her—let's see—look in the small closet off the kitchen where she keeps her ironing board and mops and stuff like that."

"All right. If I don't come back in twenty minutes, get the cops and come a-running. Got it?"

She nodded, and puffed nervously on her cigarette.

My beer case was still beneath Judy Kirkland's kitchen window. I stepped up on it, but the window was locked. I went around to the kitchen door. Locked, too. I tried the front door. No luck. I walked around the house, and I spotted a side entrance to the cellar. This door was unlocked, but it didn't get me any place—except to the cellar. I went up a short flight of steps to another door. It was locked, too, but I thought with some luck I could open it.

I took a letter from my inside coat pocket, opened the sheet of writing paper inside the envelope, and slipped it beneath the door directly beneath the key hole. Then I got out my pocket knife, which is a Rube Goldberg combination can-opener, shoe horn, ice pick, bottle opener, nail file, knife, and I don't know what all. One of the boys in the New York office had given it to me for a gag, but I had found it useful on more than one occasion. I opened the ice-pick attachment, stuck it into the key hole, wiggled it around until I pushed the key out of the lock. I heard it fall to the floor on the paper. Then I pulled the paper carefully under the door, picked up the key and unlocked the door.

I stepped inside, and I stood still and listened for a couple of seconds. The house was silent. The only sound was the ticking of a clock somewhere beyond the kitchen. I regretted that I hadn't brought a flashlight. I felt my way around the kitchen walls until I came to a door. I opened it, and I knew that I had found the closet which Sandy had mentioned. I fumbled around among mop handles, cans of floor wax, a dust pan and assorted household tools. Then my hand struck a smooth cold object, and I knew that I had found the Winchester. I took it to the kitchen window, and by the faint light from a street lamp I saw that it was the gun I had seen in Judy Kirkland's car that afternoon—a Winchester carbine, .30 caliber, lever action.

Carrying the rifle, I tiptoed towards the door. And then I stopped. There was a strange smell in the kitchen, and I sniffed the air. It was faint but I knew it was the odor of raw natural gas. I could see better in the darkness now, and I walked over to the gas range in the corner. There were six gas burners on the stove, and with my fingers I felt all the control levers. They were all turned off tight. But the faint smell of gas was still there.

I laid the gun across the kitchen table and moved silently across the kitchen. I found the door leading into the rest of the house. I opened it, and the smell of gas became stronger. Quickly, I crossed a small dining room, a living room, and by the faint light from outside I saw a stairway rising to the second floor. The stairway was carpeted, and I mounted it swiftly and silently. The smell of gas became stronger than ever.

I was in a dark hall. There were three doors opening off it. The first one was unlocked, and I peered into an empty bedroom. The dim glow from the street light outside threw a ghostly light over a neatly made bed covered with a flowered counterpane. I closed the door softly and tried the next room. This door was locked from the inside. I knelt down and put my nose to the opening at the bottom of the door. The smell of gas was strong, almost over-powering.

I stood up, debated with myself for only an instant, and then I pounded on the door with my fist. Nothing happened, and the house was deathly still. I pounded once more. No time now to use the paper-and-ice-pick trick. I backed up and threw my shoulder against the door. It held. I took three lunges before the lock finally gave away and I burst into the room.

The gas made me cough, and I ran to a window, released the catch and pushed it up. The cold November air blew in, and I turned to the bed. The light was faint, but I could see a body lying there, reposed, serene, on its back. I found the light switch then, and I flicked it on. The body on the bed didn't move.

Judy Kirkland looked like a corpse.

CHAPTER FOUR
NONE BUT THE GRAVE—

IN ONE wall of the room was an old-fashioned fireplace which had been converted to gas. There were fake clay logs resting on brass and irons, and the control valve was turned on full. The gas was hissing out into the room. I shut off the valve, sprang back to the bed, gathered Judy Kirkland up into my arms and carried her out of the room. She was clad in pale blue silk pajamas, and her body felt soft and smooth in my arms. Her long black hair, done up now in two tight thick braids, fell away from her head as I carried her down the stairs to the living room. I laid her gently on a long divan, and I switched on a floor lamp in a corner. Then I knelt beside her and laid my head to her chest. Her heart was beating very faintly.

I opened the doors and windows wide, and then I telephoned Dr. Payne. When his sleepy voice answered, I said: "Doc, this is Jim Bennett. I'm at Judy's house. She's got a big dose of gas, and her pulse is pretty low."

He didn't ask any questions. He just said, "My God!" and slammed the receiver.

I went out and turned on the porch light and waved to Sandy in my car up the street. My car lights flicked on, and I knew she had seen me. She drove down the street and parked in front of the house. As she came up the steps, I said: "Gas. I found her in her room, doors and windows locked. I called Payne."

"Poor Judy," Sandy said, and brushed past me into the house. She leaned over Judy Kirkland, felt of her pulse, said: "Quick, Jim. Help me put her on her stomach."

We turned Judy over, and Sandy knelt astride her and began pushing on the small of the unconscious girl's back and at the same time she began to swing forward and backward slowly, regulating the pressure of her hands. She was doing that when I heard a screech of brakes, followed by heavy steps on the porch. Dr. Payne burst into the room, his eyes a little wild. He was dressed in pajamas, slippers and an overcoat—nothing else. I looked at my wrist watch. It had taken him exactly four minutes from the time I had called.

He jumped to the divan, snapped at Sandy: "Let me." She moved aside, and he continued the artificial respiration. "Blankets," he said. "And coffee—hot and black." Sandy ran for the kitchen, and I pounded up the stairs for the blankets. When I came back down, Dr. Payne was still kneeling over Judy Kirkland, and although a cold wind blew through the open windows, sweat was dripping from his face. He looked quickly up at me, and his face was haggard. "She's coming around," he said.

Judy Kirkland's eyelids were flickering. I walked back to the kitchen. "Where did you learn all of that first aid stuff?" I asked Sandy.

She was watching a pan of water on the stove, waiting for it to boil. "Girl Scouts," she said. "Many years ago. How is she?"

"Coming out of it."

Without looking at me, she asked: "Why did she try to kill herself?"

That reminded me of something. "I'll tell you later," I said, and I went back through the house and up the stairs.

The lock on the door to Judy Kirkland's room was splintered, but the key was still in the lock—on the inside. I inspected the windows—there were two of them—and I found one of them was securely locked, also from the inside. It had to be, because there were no locks on the outside. And I knew that the one I had opened had been locked. I went back to the door and took the key out of the lock. It was an ordinary house key, with an open ring at one end and the conventional grooved locking device on the other—an old-fashioned key, unlike the newer short flat keys. I shook my head. What circumstance had driven Judy Kirkland to suicide? The shooting of Ralph Hollis? I doubted it. And yet it was a clear case of attempted suicide—both windows locked, and the door locked, *from the inside,* and the gas turned on full blast. I looked at the door key beneath the light. On the inside of the ring at the end of it I saw two tiny yellow flecks. They brushed off when I touched them, and I examined the key for a full minute. But it didn't get me any place. I went back downstairs.

Dr. Payne was sitting beside Judy Kirkland, and I heard him say: "You crazy little fool. Why did you do it?"

Sandy Hollis stood by with a pot of coffee in one hand and a cup in the other. The doctor held Judy's head and began to give her the coffee in slow sips. He looked at me. "Thanks, Bennett. How did you happen to find her?"

"Snooping," I said. "It's a bad habit of mine."

"A good habit," he said, softly, looking at Judy. "She owes her life to it."

Sandy said: "How is my brother, doctor?" I thought there was a hard edge to her usually pleasant voice.

Dr. Payne looked up at her. "Sandy, I meant to tell you. I saw Ralph a little while ago—I checked him before I went to bed. His fever has broken, and he is resting quietly. He's going to be all right."

Sandy sank into a chair. "I'm sorry, Doctor."

The doctor's face was suddenly grim. He looked at me. "Bennett, you're a detective. I'm sure that Judy didn't try to kill herself. Why, two hours ago, we—we made plans to get married."

"Congratulations, Doc," I said. "But it still looks like suicide to me. Windows and the door locked—from the inside, and the gas was turned on full."

"I don't care," he said, stubbornly. "Judy wouldn't do a yellow thing like that—not Judy."

And then something clicked in my brain. I got to my feet, and I moved to the door. Judy Kirkland's eyes were open, and she was watching me quietly. "What's—what's going on?" she asked, weakly.

The doctor patted her hand, said, "Sh-sh-sh," to her, and she closed her eyes.

"Sandy," I said. "You stay here with Doc and Judy. I'll be back as soon as I can."

There was fear in Sandy's eyes. "Jim! I'm going with you."

"You are like hell," I said, opening the door. "I'm going alone."

I went out and slammed the door before she could answer me. I got in my car and headed out of there, fast.

FIVE MINUTES later I pulled into the driveway of the Fortune farm. As I walked up to the porch steps I saw that Jesse Fortune's car, which had been parked in the drive earlier in the evening, was gone. I went on up on the porch and pounded on the door, waited a couple of seconds, and pounded again. And then I saw a light come on and shine down a stairway inside, and through the glass of the door I saw Eileen Fortune coming down the steps. I slipped my .38 into my overcoat pocket, and I kept my hand on it.

Eileen Fortune moved across the room inside and pressed her face against the glass, and the porch light came on. I didn't like that. I moved over, out of line from the door, and I made a motion to Eileen to open up. I heard the key in the lock, and the door swung inward. I stepped inside, quickly, and before she could move I reached out and pressed the switch which turned off the porch light. Eileen Fortune and I stood very close together in semi-darkness.

"Mr. Bennett," she said in a low voice. "What's the matter? Is Ralph—"

I didn't feel very happy. After all, she was such a pretty, clean-looking girl. "No," I said, wearily, "Ralph's all right. He's going to be fine. Doc Payne just told me."

She put a hand to her face, and she swayed towards me. I held out an arm to keep her from falling, but I kept my right arm free. She leaned against me, sobbing quietly. "I'm so glad—so glad," she said brokenly.

It was then I noticed for the first time that she was dressed only in a long nightgown, like an evening frock, with her arms and shoulders bare. Her yellow hair was done up on the top of her head, and she smelled sweet and clean, like a little girl. I moved a little away from her, but she pressed her small body more tightly against me. I said to myself: *Bennett, you old roué, this is the second time tonight you've had a half-naked girl in your arms.*

But I had work to do, unpleasant work, and I sighed. Eileen Fortune stepped back from me. "I'm sorry," she said. "But it's such a relief to know that Ralph is all right.

I've been lying upstairs awake, and wondering. Thanks so much for coming to tell me."

"That's all right," I said, lamely, "but I really came here to talk to you about something else. I'd like your father to hear it, too. Is he home?"

"Why, no," she said, "he isn't. A neighbor called him a while ago—about a sick cow. Father is something of a veterinarian, and he went to see if he could help. I expect him back soon. Will you have a cup of coffee, or a highball? I'm afraid I can't make you a Manhattan." She moved over to a table and switched on a lamp.

"Nothing, thanks," I said. "Have you been home all evening?"

She turned and looked at me, wide-eyed. She was standing in front of the light, and her slender form was silhouetted perfectly through the filmy nightgown. She saw my glance, and she crossed to a closet, took out a gabardine topcoat and flung it over her shoulders. "Yes," she said. "I've been home all evening—ever since I left the hospital. Why?" Her eyes were cool and guarded now, but I could see the vein in her throat throbbing in the light.

I wasn't getting anyplace, and I decided to let her have it. "Somebody tried to kill Judy Kirkland tonight," I said, watching her.

For a second she didn't speak. And then she said, coldly: "How?"

It wasn't the reaction I wanted. I moved backwards to the door. "Gas," I said. "But she's all right now."

"I'm glad," she said calmly. "Thanks for coming to tell me about Ralph. I'm sorry that father isn't home—but I'll tell him about Ralph—and Judy."

"All right," I said, feeling clumsy and frustrated. "Good night."

She closed the door softly behind me, and as I backed out of the drive I saw the lights in the house go off.

It was going on to two o'clock in the morning when I stopped once more in front of Judy Kirkland's house. There was a light in the front room, but when I walked in I didn't see anybody. I went back to the kitchen and I found Sandy and Dr. Payne eating cheese sandwiches and drinking beer.

Dr. Payne said: "Have a beer, Bennett."

"Not now," I said. "I'm in a hurry. Where's the high school?"

Payne looked surprised, but Sandy said: "Straight down to the courthouse, turn left, second block."

"Still the efficient secretary." I grinned at her. "How's Judy?"

"Fine," Dr. Payne said. "Thanks to you. If you had been a few minutes later—I can never repay you for that. She's sleeping quietly now." He hesitated. "Look, Bennett, maybe it's none of my business, but how did you happen to be here?"

I felt like a heel. "I'll tell you later, Doc. Save me a beer." I started for the door.

Sandy said: "Jim." She paused, and took a swallow of beer.

I turned. "Yeah?"

"There was a gun lying on the kitchen table—a .30 caliber Winchester."

"Save that, too," I said, and I went out. But before I left I saw Dr. Payne's quizzical gaze upon me.

I found the high school all right, but I had to use the flashlight in my car to locate the intersection of Crawford and Tymocktee streets. There was a light in a house on a corner, and I figured that it was the place I wanted. I didn't see any point in sneaking around, and I went right up on the front porch and pressed the bell.

Inside, I heard a man's voice singing an off-key rendition of *Star Dust: Sometimes I wonder why I spend the lonely nights....*

I waited. The singing stopped abruptly, and Earl Sarken opened the door. When he saw me, he tried to close it again, but I had a foot inside and I pushed my way on in. I stepped in quickly, and I closed the door behind me.

HE BACKED against the wall, and his glasses glittered in the light. His long thin face had a stubborn look about it. He was still wearing his fancy hunting outfit.

"Sarken," I said, "you left Dan's Grill in kind of a hurry tonight. I said I wanted to talk to you—when you were sober. Why did you run out on me?"

"Why should I talk to you?" he whispered.

"Because you're in love with Eileen Fortune, and because you're jealous of Ralph Hollis."

"I didn't shoot him," he said, still whispering.

"Prove it," I said.

He edged along the wall to a chair and sat down. He buried his face in his hands and began to sob like a baby. "I—I didn't mean—for him—to be killed," he stammered.

I heard a slight sound from the kitchen, and I turned away from Sarken and moved through the apartment. It was elegantly furnished, with over-stuffed chairs and thick rugs. I walked across a big dining room, and I could hear Sarken sobbing brokenly behind me. I entered the kitchen.

Jesse Fortune sat at a table, a half-empty bottle of whiskey in front of him. "Hello, Bennett," he said. "I wondered who came in. Have a drink?" He looked up at me, and his big red face was composed and friendly.

"Thanks," I said. "I'll be back in a minute."

I wheeled back into the dining room. But I was too late. I saw that Earl Sarken was gone. I cursed myself for a careless fool, and went to the telephone beside an ornate radio-phonograph. I called Chief of Police Wilkens. The operator rang six times before she got him out of bed.

"Chief," I said. "This is Bennett. Remember? Will you have some of your boys pick up Earl Sarken? He skipped out of his house about two minutes ago."

The Chief got excited. "Gawdamighty, Bennett, is he the blackmailer you was hunting?"

"Yep," I said. "Pick him up."

"We'll get him!" he said excitedly. "We'll get him!"

I hoped the Chief was right. I went back into the kitchen and sat down at the table with Jesse Fortune. He shoved the whiskey bottle towards me, and I poured myself a stiff drink.

Fortune said: "I figured you didn't come down here just to hunt pheasant. What've you got on Earl?"

"He's up to his neck in that Hollis shooting," I said. "What do you know about him?"

Fortune lit a long black cigar and settled back in his chair. "I've been handling a cattle deal for Earl in Cleveland today, and I came here tonight to see him about it. Earl and I always got along fine, in a business way. He's got more money than is good for him, but you can't blame a man for that. He's always been a square-shooter with me. But as for him taking a shot at Ralph—"

"I didn't say that," I said. "I'm just wondering if he *could* have been on Homer's place this morning. Do you know?"

Fortune worked his cigar around in his mouth and drummed the blunt thick fingers of his left hand on the table top. He looked at me through a cloud of blue cigar smoke, and his eyes were cool and steady. "What's it worth to you?" he said.

I leaned back in my chair. "Not much. I'm just wondering."

Suddenly he laughed. "You cops are all alike. Want to know a lot, but you never want to pay for it."

"Suit yourself," I said, finishing my whiskey. "Thanks for the drink." I stood up.

"Sit down, Bennett," Fortune said, easily. "No offense. As a matter of fact, Earl was hunting on Homer's place this morning."

"Where did you see him?" I asked. "When?"

Fortune laughed again. "You 'just wondered,' eh? I think you want to know damn bad."

"All right," I said. "I want to know this: do you think Earl Sarken tried to kill Ralph Hollis this morning because he was jealous of Ralph for taking his girl? Was Sarken near enough to Hollis to take a shot at him—at the same time that Judy Kirkland shot at a bird rising from behind Hollis?"

Fortune took the cigar from his mouth, laid it on the edge of the table, and took a drink of whiskey. "I don't know," he said seriously. "All I know is that soon after we split up, while I was walking back to my place to keep an appointment, I heard some shooting. Right after that I saw Earl walking up my lane towards the road."

"Did he see you?"

"I don't think so. I was in a hurry, and I didn't call to him."

"There were two shots," I said.

He nodded. "That's right. Almost together."

I pushed my empty glass towards him, and he filled it. "Feel like talking some more?" I asked.

He shrugged his big shoulders. "Facts are facts."

"You been here all evening with Sarken?"

"Since about eleven-thirty. I was helping a neighbor with a sick cow, and afterwards I came in to town for a drink. I met Earl at Dan's, and since I wanted to see him about this cattle deal anyway, we came here to talk it over."

"Did he leave while you were here?"

"No—wait a minute. Right after we got here, he said he had forgotten to pick up his mail. He was gone about twenty minutes, maybe a half hour."

"Took him that long to get his mail?" I asked.

Fortune took a yellow pencil out of his shirt pocket and began to tap the table with the eraser end. "I guess so," he said. "It may not have been that long."

I WAS tired of talking to him, and I was tired of stalling around waiting for the cops to bring Sarken back. And when he flashed that pencil on me, I couldn't stand it any more.

"Fortune," I said, "you're a bigger rat than I thought."

"I don't get you," he said, frowning.

"Double-crossing your prospective son-in-law like that. Tossing him in the pot to protect your own chips. Sarken wasn't on the Hollis farm this morning, and you know it. You're the one who tried to kill Ralph Hollis in order to clear the way for Sarken to marry your daughter, Eileen. You need money bad, and with Sarken for a son-in-law, you knew you could get it. You knew that if it wasn't for Ralph Hollis, your daughter would marry Sarken, and so you faked a reason for leaving the hunting party this morning, circled around, and hid in the thicket below the ravine to wait for a chance. With so many hunting in that area, an accident could easily happen. But you didn't see Judy Kirkland in the other end of the ravine until just after you shot at Ralph on the ridge. She shot at a bird at almost the same time as you shot at Ralph, only I know that her slugs didn't hit Ralph. She was standing directly below him, and the shotgun charge which hit him *slanted* across his chest—it was fired from an angle, by you. After you shot, you ducked around the far end of the thicket and lit out. But you were suspicious, so you got a rifle and hid behind the rail fence in the field above the ravine to see if anyone came back to the spot to snoop around the scene of the shooting. You took a shot at me, but you missed, and you knew then that I was on the trail of the person who shot Ralph—you knew that I knew it was not an accident. So you followed me around. In the meantime you threatened Sarken, told him what you have done to try and clear the way for him to marry your daughter, and dragged him into it—forced him to help you. Tonight you saw me go into Dan's place, and you knew Sarken was playing cards there. You went in the back way, tipped off Sarken to lead me out into the alley so that you could get a shot at me, and hid behind the ash can. Sarken scooted out and headed home, and you waited for me."

I paused. "Want to hear more, or is that enough?"

He tapped the table with his lead pencil, and he was smiling a little. "Go on, Bennett. It's very interesting."

"All right," I said. "Ever since this morning you've been worrying about Judy Kirkland—you're afraid that she might have seen you shoot at Hollis. So tonight you went to her house, sneaked into her bedroom, closed and locked the windows, turned on the gas, took one of your damn yellow pencils and stuck it through the ring end of the key to her door, tied a string to the pencil, turned the lock until the bolt was almost, but not quite, ready to click out, ran your string under the door, went outside, closed the door and pulled on the string. It doesn't take much pressure, and when you pulled the string the pencil acted as a lever and flipped the key on over, locking the door—from the *inside.* The pencil fell out of the key to the rug, and you pulled it under the door. Only I found Judy in time, and I saw the specks of yellow paint from your pencil on the inside of the ring end of the key, and I knew then what had happened. I spotted those yellow pencils in your shirt pocket when you were at Homer's last night. One of them has dents in it, made by the pressure of the ring end of the key."

Fortune held up the pencil in his hand. "Perhaps in this one," he said.

"Perhaps," I said. "That's a bad score, Fortune—two attempted murders, and two misses."

I stopped talking, and took a deep breath. Fortune sat quietly, still smiling a little. "You've got it all figured out, haven't you?" he said. "The big town dick showing off in front of the rubes. Well, you're wrong on the score—the game isn't over yet. It's two attempted murders—and *one* murder."

It was very quiet in the kitchen, and I saw death in the cold blue eyes of the man across the table. There was no time to reach for my .38, no time for anything. I saw it in his eyes and in the sudden brutal slant of his jaw. I leaped sideways and backwards from my chair, and I pushed upward on the edge of the table. The bottle and glasses crashed to the floor, and then the kitchen rocked with the blast of gunfire. I realized in that split second of time that Fortune had been holding a gun in his lap, beneath the table, all the while we had been talking. My left hip quivered and burned, and I hit the floor, hard.

Fortune was on the floor, too, and the table was on top of him. My body from my waist down was a dead weight, but I got the smooth butt of my gun in my hand, and I raised myself on one elbow. Fortune rolled clear of the table, and he fired as he rolled. His slug splintered the wooden cabinet beneath the sink behind me. I steadied my elbow on the floor and fired. My first bullet hit Fortune in the chest as he got to his knees, and it flung him violently backwards, his knees doubled under him. He uttered a hoarse cry and he twisted sideways, his big red face contorted with rage and pain. As his gun whipped around, I fired again, deliberately and slowly. The slug smacked him in just about the best place you can think of—if you're shooting for keeps—right beneath the left eye.

Jesse Fortune sighed gustily, and he pitched forward, his head in my lap.

THE CHIEF found us like that.

"Gawdamighty!" he said, and he stood staring. The big cop who had caught me in the alley behind Dan's place was standing beside him.

My hip hurt so much, and Fortune was so heavy, that I couldn't move. I couldn't do anything but just lie there, with Fortune's blood soaking my pants, and my own blood making the linoleum slippery.

"Call Doc Payne," I said. "He's at Judy Kirkland's house."

The chief jerked a thumb, and the big cop jumped for the living room. The chief leaned down, gingerly took hold of one of Fortune's ears, and tilted his head sideways. It was a mess.

The Chief mumbled to himself: "I coulda sworn that he was Jesse Fortune."

"It is," I said wearily. "Now try and get him off me."

"Gawdamighty," he muttered, as he grasped Fortune's legs and pulled him clear of me.

"Did you pick up Sarken?" I asked. My hip wasn't hurting so bad now, but it seemed to me that the kitchen floor was heaving up and down.

"Yes-sir-ee. He's outside with a couple of the boys. What you want we should do with him?"

"Bring him in here."

The big cop loomed in the doorway. "Doc's coming," he announced.

The chief said: "George, go out and bring Earl in here."

I closed my eyes, but in a minute a voice said: "Here he is, Mr. Bennett."

I looked up at Sarken standing in the kitchen doorway. He was handcuffed, and the big cop had him by the arm. He looked at me, and at the body of Jesse Fortune, and he began to tremble. He was scared blue.

"Earl," I said, and it seemed to me that my voice sounded far away, "how deep are you in this with Fortune?"

Sarken took a deep breath, tried to control himself. When he spoke, his voice was almost a whisper. He talked with his head down, not looking at me.

"I'm sorry about all this," he said. "But I couldn't help it—honest, I couldn't. I wanted to marry Eileen—I—I love her—always have, I always will..." He paused, and when he spoke again he looked at me, and his voice was stronger. "Jesse asked me, before Ralph came home, if I would loan him twenty thousand dollars, if he talked Eileen into marrying me. I said I would. I've got the money, and I wanted Eileen. He said he would 'fix it up.' But he didn't. Ralph came home, and Eileen told me they were going to get married. Her father raised hell with her, but she wouldn't listen. I gave up, but Jesse didn't. Eileen had once said that if it weren't for Ralph, she would marry me. Jesse knew that, and I guess it kind of worked on his brain. And he was really in bad. He had to have the money for a Cleveland stock syndicate by next month, or go to jail. I—"

"Why didn't you give him the money anyhow?" I asked.

"What for?" he said. "I wouldn't get it back, and I didn't like Jesse anyhow—even if he was Eileen's father. I wanted her. But I wish now I had given it to him—this—this wouldn't have happened." He dropped his head again. "Last night he started pestering me again, and so I took Eileen home and asked her once more. She refused, and I told Jesse this morning, before he went hunting. A little before noon today he came to me and told me that he had tried to kill Ralph, and that if I didn't stick by him, he'd implicate me, too. He said that he thought you were suspicious, and he told me about how he had tried to kill you, too. I think he was a little crazy. He told me to go out to the ridge this afternoon and kind of stand guard—see what was going on. That's when I met you. I was scared and worried, and I had been drinking—I didn't know what I was doing. Afterwards, I realized that my actions had made it worse for me. And then tonight Jesse told me that everyone suspected Judy, and that made me feel worse. I went to Dan's place and played poker, just before I saw you there, Jesse came in the back room and told me that you were out in front looking for me, and I should duck out the alley entrance. I told him to go to hell, and he left. But when I saw you I—I got scared—I didn't want to talk to you. And so I ducked out after all. I told the boys to stall for me, that you were an insurance salesman who had been pestering me."

Sarken's words seemed to be coming to me from down a long, dark tunnel. "Is that all?" I asked.

"Yes. I went home and I started to drink. Late tonight Jesse came home, said he had talked to you, and that everything was all right. That Ralph was recovering, and that you were convinced that Judy accidentally shot him. That made me feel good—until you came, and then I got scared again, and I knew that Jesse had lied to me."

"Fattening you up for the kill," I muttered.

I heard Sarken say: "What?"

"Tried to frame you," I said. "It doesn't matter now."

The Chief said: "What you want us to do with him?"

"Let him go." I said. "It all checks."

I didn't remember much after that. I know that Dr. Payne came, and I felt his swift, skillful hands on my body. And then there was the cold night air, a ride in a car, and Dr. Payne saying to a girl in white: "He's lost a lot of blood." And then there was the smell of ether, and a blinding white light over my head, and the faint clink of metal. And the next thing I knew I was in bed and yellow November sunlight was shining through a window.

Sandy Hollis said: "Good morning, Jim."

She was sitting beside my bed, and behind her was the tall lank form of Homer Hollis. I was conscious of a dull pain in my left hip, but otherwise I felt fine. "Hello, folks," I said, and I tried to move. But I changed my mind.

"Looks like you'll be with us for a spell, Jim," Homer said. "Reckon I'll have to get some more of that fancy booze—what is it again, now, Sandy?"

"Italian Vermouth and bourbon—we've still got plenty of bitters."

He nodded, and reached out a hand and touched my arm. "Take it easy, Jim," he said, and tiptoed out of the room.

"You crazy fool," Sandy said, and there were tears in her eyes. "Chief Wilkens told us all about it."

Dr. Payne came in, followed by a nurse. They fussed around a while, and the nurse left. The doctor said: "I don't know how to thank you..."

"Judy O.K. now?" I asked.

"Yes, she's fine—thanks to you. Ralph is fine, too. It's going to be a double wedding. We're all fine—except you. We got the bullet out of your hip—a .45—but you won't be moving around for a while yet."

"Tell me one thing, Doc," I said. "Was Judy stalling you off because she couldn't make up her mind about her old flame, Ralph?"

He looked a little startled. Then he laughed. "That's right, but she finally picked me, poor girl."

I said to Sandy: "Call the boss and tell him I fell off a bar stool and sprained my ankle and won't be at the office for a few days."

"I've already called him," she said.

"Go on. Give it to me straight."

"He said if you don't collect a fee for this job, you're fired."

"Doc," I said. "Do you need an office boy?"

Sandy held a slip of paper in front of my eyes. It was a check signed by Homer Hollis for five hundred dollars. "After all," Sandy said, "you've got to pay my salary, don't you?"

"Nuts," I said. And then I thought of something. "How's Eileen Fortune taking it—about Jesse?"

"Very bravely, so far," Sandy said. "Mom's with her now."

"By the way," Dr. Payne said. "I meant to tell you. I knew that Judy wouldn't try to—to kill herself, I found a lump on her head this morning, over her left ear. Fortune knocked her out before he turned on the gas."

"I wondered about that," I said. "Otherwise, she would probably have heard Fortune in her room."

"What'll Earl Sarken do now, I wonder?" Sandy said.

"Don't worry about him," I told her. "He's just a guy who was caught in the middle. He was willing to pay money for a bride—but not blood."

NICE, LIKE A COBRA

DETECTIVE JIM BENNETT UNCOVERS A DIABOLICAL MURDER PLOT CALLING FOR QUICK, DECISIVE ACTION!

CHAPTER ONE
CALL FOR AID

IT WAS late in the afternoon when we got back from the reefs. I helped George tie up his small launch at the dock in the yacht basin at Sand Harbor. The pickerel were running, and it had been a good day—hot, but with a cool Lake Erie breeze blowing and just enough of a swell to make the trolling perfect.

We unloaded our catch, and I made arrangements to pack some of the fish in ice to send to the boss in New York. I was pleasantly tired and relaxed, and I looked forward to a drink and dinner in the cool bar of the Harbor House.

George and I walked up the breakwater and crossed the square to the hotel. The bar was cool and dusky with the blinds drawn against the late afternoon sun. We sat down at a table in the corner, and I looked around at the familiar room with the mounted heads of fish and prints of fishing scenes. A huge colored map across the back of the bar depicted the many islands and fishing spots in this section of Lake Erie. I ordered a Manhattan, and George ordered beer.

"Too bad Bill couldn't come with us today," I said.

George nodded, said nothing. He had been unusually quiet all day, although he had seemed cheerful enough when I had called him from Cleveland and suggested that he leave his small machine-tool business long enough to take me fishing a couple of days.

George Harker was an old friend and I thought of happier days, before the war, when we had gone fishing together and sat in this bar and talked and laughed and joked together. But George's wife had died since then and his stepson, Bill, had gone to war—and returned.

"Now that Bill is out of the Army, I suppose he'll go into the business with you," I said.

The bartender brought us our drinks, and George poured out a glass of beer before he answered.

"I don't know," he said. "I want him to, and it is what his mother wanted—after he had finished school. But then the war came along. You know he left college to enlist. He expects to be discharged after this furlough. But he doesn't seem to want to talk about going into the shop with me—

he even mentioned something about heading East and going into business for himself. I can't understand it. I'm worried about him."

It was the most George had said to me at one time all day.

"After all," I said, "three years in the Pacific—"

"I know," replied George. "His nerves are bad. I know he's had a tough time, and I want him to take it easy for a while—he's only been home a week. But he's changed. Of course, he misses his mother. She died while he was overseas, you know."

I NODDED. I remembered when George had married Mabel Prentice, ten years before. I had been on a job in Mexico when she died, and I didn't hear about it until

While I held the gun on Haynes, McGuire opened the doctor's bag and there, nestled in a slot between other bottles, was the missing mouth wash.

weeks afterward. I figured George was pretty well fixed. He had his business, which must have been a gold mine during the war and I remembered that the widow, Mabel Prentice, had been rich when George married her.

"You know Jim," George continued, "ever since I married Bill's mother, and before, Bill has seemed like a son to me—the son I never had of my own. That's why I worry about him. He's been drinking too much, and he's jumpy, jittery. I finally talked him into going to Doc Haynes this afternoon for a complete check-up. I told Doc to give him a good going over."

"Has he got a girl?" I asked.

"Yes—Jean Oliver, a nice girl and a smart one. Her folks are dead, and she lives with an aunt here in town. She works in the laboratory out at the college, assists the biology professor, Hargrave. She and Bill are engaged to be married—or rather, they were, before he entered the Army."

George drained his glass of beer. "I seem to be crying on your shoulder, Jim. What time do you want to go out tomorrow?"

"Any time," I said. "Let's try some still fishing in that cove on the Canadian side."

George was looking across the room.

"Fine," he said. "Here comes Jean now."

I followed his glance and saw a girl coming across the room towards our table. She was small and slender, deeply tanned, with sun bleached blond hair. As she came up to the table I saw that her eyes were brown, and that her nose was short. She was pretty, but not too pretty. She was dressed in a short-sleeved white jersey, tan slacks and rubber-soled shoes. George and I got to our feet, and her white teeth flashed in a smile.

"Jean, this is my friend, Jim Bennett, of New York, Cleveland and points west," George said. "Jim—Jean Oliver."

I smiled, and she smiled, and we all three sat down. The bartender came over and George and I repeated our order. The girl asked for a Tom Collins, and grinned at George.

"How are you, Pop? You look burned to a crisp. Fishing today?"

"Jim and I were out on the reefs," George said. "Had some luck, too. They were hitting good."

"Speaking of luck," she said, "I had some this afternoon, too. I caught a fine specimen—a little over four feet long—the best timber rattler I've seen in several years."

"Pardon me!" I said. "Just a second there I thought I heard you say that you caught a rattlesnake this afternoon."

"But I did," she answered as she laughed. "It's part of my job—really."

"You wouldn't think it to look at her, but around here they call her the Snake Lady," George said.

"Snakes won't hurt you if you know how to handle them," she said. "The professor will be tickled with this one I got today. He's been wanting a *Crotalus Horridus* for a long time. They're rather scarce in this section, you know."

"The scarcer the better," I said, and I looked under the table. "Do you have it with you?"

She laughed again.

"No, don't worry. It is safely in the professor's hands now."

"Have you seen Bill?" George asked her.

"I saw him in the drug store early this afternoon. He said that you had pestered him into going to the doctor for a check-up. Nice going, Pop. I'm worried about that boy, but he won't listen to me. He promised to meet me here."

"Well," said George, "he didn't stand you up. Here he comes."

Two young men had entered the door and were coming towards our table. One of them was Bill, George's step-son. I knew him from the old days, and I had talked to him briefly the night before. He was a tall, good-looking boy, deeply tanned, with dark eyes and closely cropped black hair.

He was in uniform and, as he crossed the bar, his bright service ribbons glittered in a stray shaft of sunlight. On his shirt collar was the gold bar of a second lieutenant.

His companion was also tall and dark, but I guessed him to be several years older than Bill, probably close to thirty. His face was lean and tanned, and a narrow mustache accentuated the darkness of his complexion. He was dressed in gray flannel slacks and an open-necked blue sport shirt. He walked with a peculiar stiff-legged limp.

AS THEY came up to our table. Bill smiled at us, but it seemed to me that there was no humor in his eyes. George nodded at his step-son's companion.

"How are you, Greg? I want you to meet an old friend of mine, Jim Bennett. But I'm warning you, he's a big shot private detective. He's supposed to be on vacation now, but you can't trust him. Jim, this is Gregory McGuire, star reporter on your local scandal sheet."

McGuire smiled, and we shook hands.

"I've heard of you, Mr Bennett. Did a story about your handling of that West Coast job last year."

I mumbled a reply, and looked at Bill.

"Good evening, Lieutenant," I said.

"Good evening, Mr. Bennett," he mocked.

"All right—Bill, then," I said.

He laughed quickly, and motioned to the bartender. When he came over, McGuire ordered a dry Martini.

"Double whisky, soda on the side," Bill said.

George looked at me, and shook his head slightly. Bill caught the look.

"Now, now, Pop," he said, and there was a trace of irritation in his voice. "I need a bracer. I just had three teeth pulled." He felt of his jaw.

"Teeth pulled?" said George. "Didn't you see Doc Haynes?"

"Yeah, I saw him. He looked me over, asked a lot of questions. Said he couldn't find anything wrong with me. Gave me some nerve pills, and sent me to Doctor Consino to have my teeth X-rayed. Consino said there were infected roots in three of them, advised me to have them out. I told him to go ahead. They were in back."

"I told him he should have let the Army pull them—for free," Gregory McGuire said. "He's not discharged yet."

Bill drank the rest of his whisky in one swallow.

"No use monkeying around," he said.

"Does it hurt, Bill?" asked Jean Oliver.

He gave her a swift smile.

"Not much, Jeannie. Jaw's kind of sore, and I've got an awful headache. Think I'll go home and take a couple of Doc Haynes' pills and go to bed."

They talked some more, and most of the time I just listened. Bill seemed nervous, and several times I caught Jean Oliver staring moodily into her glass. Gregory McGuire seemed pleasant enough, maybe a trifle too smooth. Pretty soon someone mentioned ordering dinner, and McGuire pulled himself to his feet.

"If you'll all excuse me, I think I'll eat later," he said. "There's some work at the office I should get out first. I'll see you all later."

He nodded at me.

"Glad to have met you, Mr. Bennett." He limped across the room and out the door.

While the rest of us ate, Bill drank another whisky. When we had finished, he said:

"Come on, Jeannie. I'll take you home."

Both of them got to their feet. The girl smiled at me and at George.

"See you later, Pop," she said.

"Want to go fishing with Jim and me tomorrow, Bill?" George said.

"No, thanks," he said. "I'm playing golf with Greg." He took the girl's arm, and they went out.

I ordered more coffee.

"What's the matter with McGuire's leg?" I said to George. "Was he in the Service?"

"No. He broke his knee cap playing football. It never got right. He tried to enlist, but they wouldn't take him. He and Bill have been friends for years—grew up together. What do you make of Bill?"

"Nothing much. As you say, he's pretty jittery. He'll straighten himself out. Give him a little time. After all, Sand Harbor, Ohio, is quite a change from Iwo Jima and Okinawa."

"I guess you're right," said George. "But I hope he settles down soon. I need him."

"By the way," I said, "how are things at the shop? Reconversion bother you any?"

"You bet. Plenty. I had a lot of Government contracts canceled right after V-J Day. I figured the war would go on for at least another year and I invested a pile of money in a lot of new machinery. I'm kind of on a spot."

"Anything I can do?"

George laughed shortly.

"No—unless you can scare me up about fifty thousand bucks."

"Is it that bad?"

"Forget it. I'll work it out."

We talked a little while longer and made our plans for the next day's fishing. After George left I walked over to the bar and ordered a whisky and soda. While I drank it I thought of George and his worries, of Bill and of Jean Oliver.

I began to wonder if Bill's nervousness was due to the war, or to something else, and I thought about George and his business troubles. Then I remembered that I was on a vacation, and I tried to stop worrying about other people's troubles.

I finished my drink, bought some magazines, and went up to my room. I took a shower, climbed into pajamas, and sat in front of the open window to read. It was still light outside, and out beyond the breakwater I could see the fishing boats coming in. The streets below me were filled with summer vacationists and soldiers from a nearby Army camp.

The telephone in my room began to ring. It was George.

"Jim, can you come over right away?" he said. "Something's happened to Bill. Hurry."

CHAPTER TWO
MOUTH WASH

GEORGE HARKER lived in a big house two blocks from the lake front. The house had belonged to the widow, Mabel Prentice, before George had married her. I knew that since her death George had lived alone, eating most of his meals in restaurants, while a cleaning woman came in several times a week to straighten up for him. Now that Bill was coming home I imagined that they planned to stay in the house together, and I guessed if Bill got married all three of them would live there.

It took me about ten minutes to get dressed and to walk across town to the house.

George met me at the door, and his face was pale. He was not wearing his glasses, and his eyes looked weak and watery.

"This way, Jim," he said. "Bill's sick."

He led me upstairs and into a room where Bill was lying on a bed. He was dressed only in pajama trousers, and his long body looked leaner and darker than ever against the white sheets. His eyes were open, but he was breathing heavily. His eyes were a little bloodshot, and his whole body was bathed in sweat. His face glistened with it. He looked at me, and he tried to grin.

"Have you called a doctor?" I asked George.

"Yes. He's on the way."

"What happened?"

"I don't know. He was already home when I got here. I sat down to read the paper. I heard Bill upstairs in the bathroom—water running, and the slamming of drawers. Pretty soon, maybe fifteen or twenty minutes, he called down to me. I came up, and found him lying there on the bed. He said he was sick. Then he kind of passed out. I ran downstairs, called Doc Haynes, then I called you."

I spoke to the boy on the bed.

"How you feeling now?"

"Not—so good, Jim," he gasped.

"Did you fall, or strike your head?"

"No—took—couple—those pills—" He stopped, his jaws working soundlessly.

I bent over the bed and felt of Bill's head. I could find no marks or bruises which would indicate a blow. I felt his wrist for his pulse. It was feeble. His eyes were half closed, and they glittered brightly. His ordinarily thin face looked a little puffy. He muttered something, but the words were unintelligible.

The doorbell rang.

"That'll be Doc," George said, and he went downstairs.

I walked into the bathroom and looked around. On the bowl under the mirrored door of a wall cabinet was a toothbrush, a tube of toothpaste, a small open bottle containing a brownish colored liquid and a small white envelope such as doctors use to dispense capsules and pills. A corner of the envelope was torn off. I shook a couple of tiny white pellets into my hand and put them to my pocket. On a corner of the envelope was printed, ROBERT H.

HAYNES, M.D, and scrawled across it in blue ink were the words, "For nerves—2 or 3 at bedtime."

I picked up the bottle of brown liquid and screwed the cap back on it. On the label was printed, VICTOR D. CONSINO, D.D.S. Beneath this was written, "Rinse mouth three times daily, full strength."

I heard George and the doctor come up the stairs and enter the bedroom. I put the bottle down, and followed them. The doctor was standing by the bed. He was young, about thirty-five, I guessed, with a round cheerful face and thinning blond hair. He was dressed in a well cut tan gabardine suit and was a little on the chunky side, with wide thick shoulders.

He examined the boy on the bed very carefully, asked quick questions of George, felt the boy's pulse, took his temperature. He got out a hypo needle and jabbed it into Bill's bare shoulder. Then he stepped back and shook his head.

"I don't know," he admitted. "At first glance it looks like a cerebral hemorrhage. Lot of the symptoms, but Bill's too young for that—unless he struck his head against something, and I can't find anything like that."

"He took some of those pills you gave him," I said.

Dr. Haynes swung his head at me.

"Those pills are merely a sedative. They won't hurt him—unless he took a lot of them."

"Doctor Haynes, this is Jim Bennett, a friend of mine," George said.

The doctor nodded.

"How many would be a lot?" I asked.

"Fifteen or twenty," he answered. "Why? Do you think—?"

"No," I said. "He didn't take that many."

THE DOCTOR looked at me steadily for a second before he turned to George.

"He's resting easier now. Keep cold cloths on his head—better still, an ice bag. I don't think he's in any immediate danger now, but if he appears to get worse, call me. I've got to go back to the office, but I'll be back as soon as I can get away. Take his temperature and pulse every half hour."

He picked up his bag and started for the door. He paused.

"I'd like to wash my hands," he said.

George nodded towards the bathroom.

"Sure. In there."

Dr. Haynes went in and closed the door. I heard water running, and in a couple of minutes he came out. He picked up his bag and nodded at me.

"Be sure and call me if you think it is necessary," he said to George, and went down the stairs. I heard the front door slam, and then the sound of his car starting out in front.

"I'll get some cold towels," I said to George. "If you've got an ice bag, better dig it out." I went into the bathroom, took a towel from a wall cabinet, and turned to the wash bowl. As I turned on the water I realized that something was missing from the top of the bowl. The envelope of pills was still lying there, but the bottle of mouthwash was gone.

I soaked the towel in cold water, wrung it out, and went into the bedroom. George was holding a watch in his hand and feeling his stepson's pulse. I laid the towel on the boy's head. His eyes were closed, and he seemed to be resting more easily, but I thought that his face looked even more puffy than it had earlier.

"There's nothing I can do here right now," I said to George. "I'll be back in a little while."

"All right, Jim," George said. "Thanks for coming up. I guess the fishing is off for tomorrow."

"Forget it," I said. "See you later."

I went down the stairs and out the front door. It was four blocks to the hotel, and I made it in about three minutes. I went up to my room, fished my .38 out of my bag, spun the cylinder to make sure it was full of slugs, stuck it in my inside coat pocket, and went back down to the lobby. The clerk told me that Dr. Haynes' office was across the street, upstairs, over a drug store.

I found the stairway leading up to his office without any trouble. On the second floor I spotted a ground glass door painted with the doctor's name, and I obeyed the sign which said, "Walk In." There were five people waiting in the outer office. Four women and a man. A sign on a door leading to an inner office read, "The Doctor is IN." I heard voices from beyond the door, and so I eased my hundred and ninety pounds into one of the straight chairs which lined the wall.

In about five minutes the door opened and Dr. Haynes poked his head out and looked around. One of the women got to her feet. Then the doctor spotted me. He registered surprise. I got up.

"May I see you for a minute, Doctor?" I said. "It's very urgent."

He hesitated.

"Do you mind, Mrs. Lapham?" he said to the woman.

Mrs. Lapham minded, but she sat down again. I walked through the door, and the doctor closed it behind me. Jean Oliver was standing by a desk in the middle of the room. She was still wearing the white jersey and the blue slacks.

"Hello, Miss Oliver," I said.

She nodded, but she didn't smile.

"What's wrong?" Dr. Haynes asked. "Is Bill worse?" There was a red smear on his upper lip, just under his nose.

"May I speak to you—alone?" I said.

"Don't mind Miss Oliver," he said. "She assists me quite frequently—blood tests, analyses, things like that. Quite competent, too." He grinned at her.

"All right," I said. "I came for that bottle of mouth wash."

He looked startled. Then he straightened his face.

"Oh, the mouth wash," he said. "I took it along to have it analyzed. Why do you want it?"

"For the same reason, maybe—and just because you took it."

"I see," he said "Well, I'll put your inquisitive mind at rest. I don't think the mouth wash has anything to do with Bill's illness, but I don't want to overlook any possibilities. So I asked Miss Oliver to come over and analyze it for me."

I THOUGHT this over for a moment or two.

"What about the pills Bill took?" I asked.

"I know what they contain," he snapped. "Look here—"

"Never mind, Doctor," Jean Oliver cut in. "I should have told you that Mr. Bennett is a detective. He follows up clues. In his memoirs this hair-raising episode will no doubt be called, 'The Case of the Missing Mouth Wash.'"

I turned on my stern look.

"Miss Oliver, you do not seem concerned over Bill's condition."

"Why do you think I'm here?" she flung at me. "If I can help to find out what is wrong with him by analyzing the contents of a bottle of mouth wash, that is what I want to do. Doctor Haynes has assured me that Bill is in no immediate danger."

"I hope he is right," I said, and turned to the doctor. "I'll take that bottle now."

He opened a desk drawer, took out the bottle, still filled with the brownish fluid, and handed it to me.

"Thanks," I said. "I'll return it to you shortly—or not at all. In the meantime, you'd better wipe that lipstick off your kisser."

He reddened, and was fumbling for a handkerchief as I closed the door behind me.

Mrs. Lapham gave me a mean look as I came out.

"You're next, madam," I said, and went out into the hall.

In the drug store downstairs I found a phone booth and called the office of the dentist, Consino. I got no answer, so I called his home. Still no answer, so I checked his address in the telephone directory and headed out of the store.

As I passed the newspaper and magazine racks near the entrance, I saw Gregory McGuire idly standing there looking over the titles. He had changed to a dark blue double-breasted suit, and he had a Cleveland Plain Dealer under his arm. He caught sight of me.

"Hello, there," he said.

"Hello, McGuire," I said. "Did you know that Bill is sick?"

"No. What's the matter?"

"Don't know. George found him on the bed a little while ago. Just sort of keeled over."

"Did George call the doctor?"

"Yeah. Haynes was up, but he can't figure it out. Said it might be a cerebral hemorrhage, but he don't know. Is Haynes considered a good man?"

"Yes," replied McGuire. "He has a large practice. He's been in Sand Harbor about six or seven years."

"What about the dentist, Consino?"

"I don't know, exactly," he answered. "Some people swear by him. Others say they wouldn't let him work on their dog. He drinks a lot. Lives alone out along the lake. He came to town about the same time as Doc Haynes. Quite a character, sort of a soldier of fortune before he went to medical school. I understand that he decided to become a dentist quite late in life."

"That's a pretty complete description," I said. "Does Haynes usually recommend Doctor Consino to his patients who need dental attention?"

"I've heard that he does," said McGuire.

"Is Consino a good dentist?"

"One of the best, they say—when he's sober." McGuire moved towards the door. "Is there anything I can do to help Bill?"

"You might go up and see if George needs anything. I'll be there shortly, and Doctor Haynes said he would be back."

"Don't you think that maybe Bill should be in the hospital?"

"Haynes didn't say anything about it," I answered.

"I'd better get up there," he said. "See you later."

We left the store together, and McGuire limped away in the direction of George's house. Suddenly a thought struck me. It was a mean, suspicious thought, but it hit me hard, all of a sudden.

"Hey, McGuire!" I called.

He stopped and turned. I walked up to him.

"Who's the county recorder?" I asked. He looked at me, a puzzled expression on his face.

"The county recorder? Why, Abe Humphrey."

"Thanks," I said, and walked away.

I found a taxi down the street, and told the driver to take me to Dr. Consino's house.

CHAPTER THREE
EVIL SUSPICIONS

CONSINO'S PLACE was small, about a mile from town, close to the beach. It looked like more of a summer cottage than a house, and was at the end of a long dirt road leading off the Toledo-Cleveland highway. As the taxi bumped over the rutty road lined with high swamp grass, I could see the gleam of the lake through the trees, and the last red streaks of the sun over beyond Put-In-Bay. The taxi stopped in front of the cottage and I got out and pounded on the door of the screened porch, but I got no answer.

I pounded some more.

"Dangit!" a voice called. "Around here—in back!"

I motioned to the taxi driver to wait, and walked around the cottage through the knee-high grass and weeds. In the back of the place there was a cement terrace facing the lake. Except for the distant hum of traffic on the highway it was very quiet, and I could hear the sound of the waves on the beach fifty yards away.

A man was sitting in a canvas deck chair on the terrace. He was about fifty years old, medium sized. I could see that he had thick gray hair, a wide flat nose, a wide flat mouth and a square jaw. He was dressed in wrinkled white linen slacks and a short-sleeved open-necked shirt. He was wearing big, goggle-like dark sun glasses. In his hand was a thin-stemmed cocktail glass, and on the terrace beside him was a silver shaker glistening with beads of moisture.

"Doctor Consino?" I asked.

He appeared to be watching the horizon, and he didn't turn his head when I spoke.

"This is my night off," he said, "Have a drink?"

"No, thanks." I said. "I'm in a hurry. My name is Bennett. I'm sorry to bother you on your night off, but you pulled some teeth for Bill Prentice this afternoon and you gave him some mouth wash to use. Is this it?" I held the bottle around in front of his face.

He peered at it intently, still not looking at me.

"Take off your sun glasses," I said. "The sun's down."

"Can't stand the light," he replied. "My eyes are weak. A cobra spit in 'em once. Been weak ever since."

"Sorry," I said. "Can you read the label?"

"Certainly. Just a simple astringent and antiseptic. Give it to all my patients after extractions."

"All right," I said. "Something caused Bill Prentice to keel over tonight. He was semi-conscious when I left him, maybe he's worse now. Something caused it and I'm checking on this bottle of mouth wash because somebody swiped it out of George Harker's bathroom tonight right after Bill got sick."

For the first time Dr. Consino turned his head and looked at me. He peered upward through his absurd dark glasses.

"What are Bill's symptoms?" he asked.

"Face a little puffy, eyes bloodshot, pulse weak, excessive perspiration, partial paralysis."

"Snake bite," he said, promptly, still peering upwards at me. "Where did the snake bite him? In the face? The swelling there would indicate that."

"Look," I said gently. "A snake didn't bite him—unless there was a snake in his bathroom." And then something clicked in my brain. "The devil!" I almost yelled. "Listen to me, Doc. What would happen to a man if he rinsed his mouth after having some teeth extracted—and he used a mouth wash with snake venom in it?" I was so excited that I began to shake a little.

But Dr. Consino was again studying the horizon.

"I'm thirsty," he announced. "Fetch me that quart milk bottle from the ice box."

I was suddenly in a tearing hurry, but I knew that I had to humor this man if I was to find out what I wanted to know. I almost ran to the back door of the cottage, entered the kitchen and opened the door of an old fashioned ice box. Leaning against a half melted cake of ice was a milk bottle filled with a light amber colored fluid. It was the only milk bottle I saw, so I grabbed it and carried it to Dr. Consino. He held out his glass, and I filled it with the amber fluid. He held it up to the fading light.

"No olive," he said reproachfully.

I smelled the contents of the milk bottle, and then I took a sip. It was Martini cocktail, very cold and very dry.

"Cobra venom is just about the color of a dry Martini—maybe a little darker," said Dr. Consino. "Years ago, when I was in the British army in Africa, one of them spit at me—I mean a cobra. Got me right in the eyes. They have been weak ever since."

HE WAS rambling. So I brought him back to the subject which as on my mind.

"You told me that," I said. "What would happen to a man—"

"If the venom were strong enough," he broke in, "the man would die—unless he received prompt treatment. It doesn't matter how the venom gets into his bloodstream. I recommend an injection of antivenomous serum. Isn't the lake beautiful tonight?"

"Doctor, do you have any idea how snake venom could get into Bill Prentice's mouth wash?" I said.

"Hanged if I know. I wish I had some olives."

"Doctor Consino, listen. This is serious. I don't know if Bill is suffering from the effects of snake poison or not. But I've got to find out. If he is, I've got to find some snakebite serum."

"Give him the serum anyhow. It won't hurt him."

"Look, Doctor. Can you tell me if there is snake venom in this mouth wash?"

"Nope. You might try drinking it."

"Where can I get it tested?"

"Doctor Haynes has a well equipped laboratory."

"Where else?"

He looked up at me again.

"Oh, choosey, eh?"

"Yeah."

"Try Hargrave—at the college. He might even have some serum. He uses it in experiments. Young man, I think you need a drink."

"Very true," I said. "But I gotta go. Thanks. I may see you later."

I ran around the cottage to the taxi. As I climbed in, I heard Consino yell:

"Bring some olives when you come back!"

"Back to town," I told the driver. "And stop at the first telephone."

He grinned at me.

"Was Doc sober?"

"No," I said. "About half."

It was almost dark. We headed slowly down the rough road towards the main highway. A cool breeze blew in from the Lake and through the open cab windows. I saw a big illuminated stop sign at the highway intersection ahead, and the taxi slowed down. It was barely moving when I heard the shots from the woods on my right. I felt the hot breath of the slugs as they burned past my eyes. The driver yelled and the cab jerked to a stop.

I ducked low, unlimbered my .38, opened the door, and slid out to the road. I heard a crashing in the underbrush in the woods to the right of the road, and I pumped a couple of slugs in that direction. The crashing stopped, and I waited a minute, my gun ready.

Nothing happened. I didn't like the idea of making a cops and robbers chase of it—not in the woods at night—and anyhow, I didn't have time. I got back into the cab. The driver had scooted out of his side and was crouched in the road close to the running board.

"All right," I said. "Let's get out of here."

"Yes, *sir!*" he said, and the cab's tires skidded in the gravel as we took off.

Back in town we stopped in front of the drug store below Dr. Haynes' office. I went in to the phone booth and called George Harker's house.

Jean Oliver answered the phone.

"How's Bill?" I asked.

"Not very good." Her voice sounded as though she had been crying. "His pulse is weaker, and—" She paused.

"Is Dr. Haynes there?"

"Yes. He's doing all he can."

I asked her to let me talk to George.

"Pop isn't here right now," she said.

"Where is he?" I asked, and the mean, suspicious thoughts again flooded my brain.

"He went out to buy an ice bag."

"How long has he been gone?"

"I don't know," she almost wailed. "Maybe a half an hour. Goodby."

The click of her receiver hurt my ear drum. I hung up and looked up the number of Professor Hargrave's house. His wife said he was still at the college. I thanked her, thumbed through the directory again, and found the number of the residence of Abe Humphrey, the county recorder. The mean thoughts were still in the back of my head.

ABE HUMPHREY was a friendly, talkative gentleman, and he readily told me all I wanted to know.

"Mabel Harker's will? The whole town knows it. It was even in the paper after she died. She left her whole estate—value of about a hundred thousand including her house, other properties and securities—to her son, Bill. Al Prentice left her pretty well fixed.

"After she married George she even made him sign a waiver that in the event of her death all of her holdings went to Bill—and poor George, her lawful, wedded husband. I always said George was crazy for signing off that way."

I hesitated a second before I asked my next question. George Harker was a good friend of mine. But in my business I have to do a lot of things I don't like to do. But I had to find out.

"Mr. Humphrey," I said. "What if Bill should die?"

"In that case, George automatically gets the whole shooting match."

"Thanks," I said wearily, and hung up. My body felt like a chunk of lead.

I walked out of the drug store and climbed into the waiting taxi.

"Still want me for a fare?" I asked the driver.

"Sure. Where to?"

"To the college. I gotta find Professor Hargrave. And make it fast."

We went fast. The college was on the south side of town, but we made it there in about three minutes. Most of the buildings were dark, but the driver apparently knew where Professor Hargrave could be found. He turned into a driveway which ran between neatly trimmed hedges and came to a stop beneath a lighted window.

"The lab," he said. "Here's where the Professor hangs out."

I climbed a short cement stairway and knocked on a door. In a minute it was opened by a little man with a gray mustache and gray slicked down hair.

"Come in, come in," he said, and immediately left me and went back to a bench and an array of bottles, test tubes and rows of labeled containers. It looked like a laboratory in a Boris Karloff movie, only smaller.

I followed the Professor over to the bench.

"I'm sorry to bother you, Professor, but it's really pretty important," I said.

He was peering into a microscope.

"Yes, yes. What is it?"

I put the bottle of mouth wash on the bench where he could see it.

"I think there is snake venom in that mouth wash," I said. "Bill Prentice had some teeth pulled this afternoon. He used that mouth wash this evening. Right now Bill is a very sick boy—maybe dying."

Professor Hargrave jerked up, hit his head.

"Why didn't you say so? Bill Prentice is a fine boy—even if he is going to marry the best assistant I ever had." He picked up the bottle, and started for an adjoining room.

"Hey," I called after him. "Check these while you're at it." I dropped in his hand the pills I had taken from the envelope which Dr. Haynes had given Bill.

He hurried into the next room with the pills and the bottle.

"Wait where you are," he called over his shoulder.

It didn't take him very long. In a little while he came out. He had the bottle of mouth wash in one hand, and a small leather case in the other.

"Come on, come on!" he snapped. "We've got to get this serum to Bill right away."

"You've got some snake bite serum?"

"Yes, yes. Very lucky. I use it in toxicology experiments. The liquid in this bottle is saturated with the venom of the *Crotalus Horridus*—extremely toxic. The pills are a simple sedative—harmless, unless taken in quantity. What are Bill's symptoms?"

As we went out the door and got into the waiting taxi, I told the Professor all about Bill and how long ago he had used the mouth wash. It had been a little over an hour since I had left George's house.

The Professor made a clucking sound with his tongue.

"That's not good—especially since the poison was introduced more or less directly into his blood stream. It's fantastic. How in the world—"

"Yeah," I grunted. "That's what I want to find out."

CHAPTER FOUR
ANTI-VENOM INJECTION

THE TAXI didn't take long to get us to George's residence. I paid the taxi driver and told him not to wait. The professor and I went into the house and up the stairs.

There was quite a crowd in Bill's bedroom—George, Jean Oliver, Gregory McGuire and Dr. Haynes. Jean Oliver was down on her knees applying towels to Bill's face and head. Bill was lying very quietly now. His face and lips were swollen grotesquely, and he was shiny with perspiration. The girl continually wiped a thin trickle of blood from his lips. Dr. Haynes was holding a stethoscope to Bill's chest. As we came in, I saw him look up at George and shake his head slightly. Jean Oliver caught the look, and it seemed to me that her face went a shade paler.

Professor Hargrave walked into the room. I stood in the doorway.

"Doctor Haynes, with your permission, Professor Hargrave is going to administer some anti-venomous serum," I said. "Will you assist him?"

The doctor jerked up his head, and the rest of the persons in the room looked at us for the first time. For an instant no one spoke, no one moved. It was like a movie suddenly stopped. Professor Hargrave stepped forward, opened his leather case and took out a hypodermic needle. Dr. Haynes took a step backward. There was a stubborn look on his face.

The Professor was brisk, businesslike. He adjusted a glass tube containing a pale fluid to the hypo needle. Then he uncorked a small bottle, and I could immediately smell the alcohol. He dipped the point of the needle into the alcohol and handed the outfit to Dr. Haynes.

"Will you be so kind, Doctor? You are familiar with the technique? Subcutaneous injection. Two cubic centimeters in his back, between the shoulder blades. Also, two cubic centimeters in the abdomen in the same manner. Do you think it advisable to also administer the serum intravenously?"

Dr. Haynes stood still. He made no move to take the needle.

"What kind of serum is that?" he asked harshly.

Professor Hargrave looked surprised.

"Why, anti-venomous—snake-bite serum, Doctor. Very fortunate that I had some on hand. It was sent to me by a friend at the institute at Sao Paulo, in Brazil. We may be too late, but we can try. We should also use a ligature and suction, but unfortunately the point at which the venom has entered Lieutenant Prentice's blood stream—through open tooth cavities in his gums—makes such treatment almost impossible. Let us hope that the serum alone neutralizes the neurotoxic element. Please, Doctor. Quickly."

Dr. Haynes' face was red.

"Are you crazy? What makes you think he is suffering from snake poison?"

"Dr. Haynes," I said, "there was snake venom in Bill's bottle of mouth wash."

"Ridiculous!" he snapped, and moved towards the door. I stepped in front of him. He turned to George.

"George, I'm sorry, but I cannot be responsible," he said "I'll have no part in this—this mumbo-jumbo."

George looked at me for the first time.

"It's up to you, Jim. Do you think it will help Bill?"

"It will help, if anything can," I said.

"My God!" burst out the professor. "It won't hurt him, and it may save his life."

George's face was pale and drawn as he nodded to the professor.

"Go ahead," he said.

"I'll help," Gregory McGuire said, and he stepped to the bedside. He and the professor turned Bill over on his back. While they worked, I leaned against the door and lighted a cigarette. Dr. Haynes just stood there, watching. He didn't know whether to choke or wind his watch. Jean Oliver stood beside George and watched the professor and McGuire.

The professor straightened up and spoke to the girl.

"Get that drainage tube from my case, and the small suction pump. We'll try and clear his mouth of the blood and toxic matter. I will also need some warm water, and an atomizer. I want to make a mild solution of permanganate crystals."

She nodded, and busied herself obeying his instructions. She brought in a pan of warm water and put it on the table beside the bed. George Harker just sat and watched. When I looked at George, I thought of the ice bag Jean had told me he had gone out to get.

I glanced around the room and spotted the bag lying on the floor beneath the bed, where the professor had apparently placed it to get it out of his way. I smiled, and tried to make the night's happenings connect up in my mind, but they wouldn't jell.

DOCTOR HAYNES suddenly made up his mind to leave. He picked up his bag. I chose that moment to make my little speech.

"George, I've done all I can," I said loudly, so that all in the room could hear me. "It's now in the hands of the police."

"The police?" asked George. As he looked up at me his face seemed paler and more drawn.

"Yes, George," I said. "There's no use kidding ourselves. Somebody put that poison in Bill's mouth wash. If Bill dies, it's murder. If he lives, it's still a tough rap."

"Bill didn't have any enemies," Jean Oliver said.

"Somebody tried to kill him," I insisted.

"This is a lot of nonsense," Dr. Haynes said. "Under the circumstances, I think it best that I leave. Jean, are you coming along?"

"No," she said.

"Professor, will you hand me the bottle of mouth wash?" I said. "It's the only evidence we have. I want to take it to the police."

Professor Hargrave straightened up from leaning over the bed.

"What? Oh, the mouth wash. Certainly, certainly." He peered around him, felt in his pockets, glanced at the table by the bed. The bottle was nowhere in sight.

"It's in this room, and I'm going to find it," I said. "I'll start with you, McGuire."

"Okay," he said. "But I'm sure I haven't it."

"All right," I said, "I'll take your word for it—at least, for the present. Miss Oliver?"

She turned from bathing Bill's head and gave me a quick, scornful glance. She said nothing.

"I didn't see it, Jim," George said.

"Dr. Haynes?"

"Of course not," he snapped. "Why should I take it?"

"I'm sorry. Doctor, but I'm afraid I'll have to search you. I'm sure you'll understand—since we seem to have had this same trouble before this evening."

I stepped towards him.

"Don't touch me, you cheap dick," he said, evenly. "You haven't the authority."

"Maybe not," I said, and I slipped my .38 from my inside coat pocket and pointed it at his middle. The room was suddenly very quiet.

"I'll start with your bag," I said.

For a second I thought he was going to make a dive for me. But he didn't. He just glared.

"McGuire," I said, "will you be kind enough to look in Doctor Haynes' bag for me?"

Gregory McGuire limped quickly forward. He took the bag from the doctor's hand.

"Excuse me, Doc," he said, and opened it. Nestled in a slot between the rows of small bottles was the missing bottle of mouth wash. I took it out, and put it in my pocket.

"Thank you, McGuire," I said.

The doctor's face was expressionless. He said nothing. I looked around at the rest of the persons in the room. Something wasn't right. The actors in this little drama were all playing the wrong parts. Or at least, they seemed all wrong to me. They were all looking at me, and I thought fast.

I stepped to the door.

"George, do you mind if I use your car to drive to the police station?" I said.

"Of course not, Jim," he said. "It's down in the garage. The keys are in it."

"Thanks," I said, and I stepped into the hall.

Gregory McGuire spoke up.

"I'll drive you, Mr. Bennett. My car is down in front."

"So is mine," said Haynes, suddenly. "I'm leaving now. You can ride with me."

It was beginning to be silly—like Alphonse and Gaston. I grinned.

"Thank you, gentlemen, but I'll take George's car," I said. "I want to come back here, anyhow."

Professor Hargrave glanced up from beside the bed.

"His pulse is stronger," he announced. Dr. Haynes looked interested, but he said nothing.

"Good," I said. "The serum seems to be working."

I NODDED at the room in general and went down the hall to the stairs and through the house to the kitchen. I let myself out the back door and walked halfway around the house to get a look at the cars parked out in front. There were three of them, belonging, I guessed, to Dr. Haynes, McGuire and Jean Oliver.

I hurried back across the dark back yard to the garage. The doors were standing open, and I went in and turned on the headlights of George's sedan. I had to work fast.

By the reflected light I looked quickly around the garage. Leaning in a corner I saw what would serve my purpose—a thick roll of old carpeting. I put it on the front seat of the car behind the wheel and stuck my hat on top of it. I figured it would look a lot like a man behind the wheel to anyone peering into the garage from outside. Then I checked the ignition switch to make sure it was turned off, and I moved the gear shift lever into neutral.

Then I crouched down beside the running board with the door open so that I could reach the starter button with my hand. I got my .38 out, and I squatted there on the floor and waited.

I heard the front door of the house slam, and the sound of a car being started. McGuire, Jean Oliver or the doctor leaving, I thought, and I waited some more. Nothing happened. I began to wonder if my little trap was all set and baited for nothing.

And then I heard a soft sound—the careful closing of the back door of George's house. I pressed my finger against the starter button of the car. The starter began to grind loudly. I let up on the button, pressed down on it again. Then I saw a dark shadow flit past the garage doors. I let up on the starter, squared myself around, and ducked lower.

There was a sudden hammering blast, and the windows of the car shattered into bits. My hat, which had been resting on top of the roll of carpeting, fluttered to the floor beside me, and the carpeting jumped as the slugs thudded into it. I leaped for the garage doors, and as I did so another shot crashed through the car.

This time I saw the bright flash of flame, and I cut loose with my .38. I heard a voice cry out in pain, and I fired twice more before I jumped clear of the garage.

In the gravel driveway lay the body of a man. I leaned down and turned it over. There wasn't much light, but I saw that it was Gregory McGuire.

CHAPTER FIVE
THE MOTIVE

A COUPLE of my slugs had caught him—one in the chest, and the other in his left side. As I kneeled beside him, he opened his eyes.

"You win," he said. "Neat trick." He coughed, and blood ran out of his mouth.

"Quick, McGuire," I said. "The cops will be here in a minute. How did you get the snake poison in Bill's mouth wash?"

He tried to grin up at me, and he coughed again.

"Easy. I was out with Jean this afternoon. I often went with her, before Bill came home. After we caught that rattler, we milked it, took its venom, and put the venom in a bottle. I carried it.

"I was supposed to give it to the professor, along with the snake. I gave him the snake, but I kept the bottle of poison. Don't know why. Morbid, maybe. Maybe subconscious intention. You're a detective—is that the way murders begin at first, before they even know they are going to do it?"

"Yeah," I said. "Sometimes."

He coughed some more.

"But on with the story," he said. "I want it straight for the papers that a dying man has confessed to the snake murder.

I had the poison in my pocket when I met Bill outside the hotel tonight, just before we met you. He told me about having the teeth pulled and he showed me the bottle of mouth wash which Consino had given him.

"I watched him put it in his car before we went into the hotel and an idea hit me. The combination was too good to pass up—teeth pulled, raw open gums, mouth wash, snake venom. You know the rest. I left the hotel before the rest of you, took the bottle of mouth wash from Bill's car, poured some out, filled the bottle with snake venom. Simple, like that."

"Why?" I asked. "Because of Jean Oliver?"

"Certainly. Why else? I hated Bill Prentice even before he went away. I hated him because of Jean, because she loved him. It was the old fashioned triangle. While he was away I had her all to myself. It was swell. Oh, she was true to her soldier. She liked me, all right—like a brother. You know. And when he came home. I knew it was all over. I knew I didn't have a chance as long as Bill was alive. So I tried to kill him. Silly of me, wasn't it?"

"Did you take a couple of shots at me tonight out at Consino's?" I asked.

"Yes." McGuire's voice was getting weaker, and his eyes were thin slits in his face. "I followed you after I saw you in the drug store. I parked my car on the beach and watched you from the woods, saw you show the bottle to Consino, knew you were on my trail. I hid in the woods along the road—tried to kill you."

He stopped, coughed, and looked up at me. His eyes glittered in the dim light.

"I wish I had killed you," he said.

I shivered in the warm night air.

"Yeah," I said, "I guess you do."

Lights were coming on in the houses all around us, and I heard a car coming up the street—fast. Gregory McGuire stretched out on the gravel and sighed. He closed his eyes. I put my hand on his blood-soaked shirt. His heart was still beating. I got to my feet as the police car pulled up to the curb.

It was quite a mess after that. I had a lot of explaining to do. They took me down to the station and McGuire was hauled to the hospital. The cops told me later that he signed a confession, and that they thought he would live. They finally let me go back to George's house.

Professor Hargrave and Jean Oliver were still there, and Bill was showing steady improvement. The serum seemed to be doing its job.

The professor explained that the venom in the mouth wash was that of a timber rattlesnake, a comparatively small species found in the central states and on the shores and islands of Lake Erie. Its poison, he said, was not as deadly as that of the big diamondbacks of the Southwest, and Bill had gotten only a small dose in his system through the raw tooth cavities in his jaws. Nevertheless, as the professor pointed out, it could have been fatal if not treated within a few hours.

Down in George's kitchen, over beer and cheese sandwiches, Jean Oliver confirmed McGuire's story of how he had procured the venom.

JEAN SAID that McGuire had asked to go along with her, pleaded that it would be the last chance he would have to be with her, that he was going away.

She consented, and when they caught the snake he had wanted to "milk" it on the spot. He helped her pin the snake down while she pressed on the poison glands behind the snake's jaws and caught the venom dripping from the snake's fangs in a small bottle. McGuire had promised to deliver the snake and the venom to Professor Hargrave, who used the poison in serum-making experiments of his own.

I told her what McGuire had said about being in love with her. She admitted that she had been aware of McGuire's feeling for her, and had attempted to keep him from seeing her. But he had insisted on her company, hoping that she would forget Bill and fall in love with him.

"I felt sorry for him, until I learned that he was writing lies to Bill, telling Bill that I was untrue to him," she said. "He caused plenty of trouble. After all, Bill was far away, and Gregory was his best friend. I'll never forgive Gregory for that. Poor Bill had enough on his mind, out there in the Pacific, and he didn't know what to believe. That was what worried Bill, even after he got home.

"I didn't believe Gregory's story about his going away, but I let him go along with me today because I wanted to try and persuade him to tell Bill that he had been lying about me. But he wouldn't do it. He said if he couldn't have me, Bill wouldn't have me, either. I think he was a little mad."

"And that is why you didn't say anything to us about being with McGuire this afternoon?" I asked.

"Yes," she said. "I was afraid Gregory would mention the snake, but he didn't"

"Naturally not," I said. "He had made up his mind to try and poison Bill by then. Had it occurred to you that if Bill had died, an autopsy would have pinned it on you?"

She shivered slightly.

"Let's not talk about it. It's all over now. The professor let me talk to Bill a little while ago. We're getting married as soon as he is well."

"In that case, I guess I can forget about seeing your lipstick on Doctor Haynes' face," I said, grinning at her.

She flushed, but before she could answer, Haynes walked into the kitchen.

"I heard you, Bennett," the doctor said. "Don't blame Jean. I've admired her for a long time—Bill's a very lucky guy. No harm in making a friendly pass, is there, just to see if it works? I kissed her, all right, but I didn't get any cooperation—hang it."

Jean Oliver laughed.

"You're still my favorite doctor," she said.

"It's all over now, Doc," I said. "Why were you so anxious to get hold of that mouth wash?"

His face got red, and he looked embarrassed.

"Bennett, I guess I owe you an apology for my actions. I thought you were just meddling in something which didn't concern you. And I really didn't think Bill was in a serious condition, not until his heart action began to slow down. I admit now I was wrong. But, good grief, what doctor would think of snake poison in a man's home?" He sighed, and poured himself a glass of beer.

"It's kind of a long story, but I'll make it as brief as I can," he continued. "Dr. Consino was an old friend of my father's. When my father died, he sort of looked after me. In fact, he even paid part of my way through medical school. He's knocked around a lot, all over the world. Suddenly, just after I had entered medical school, he decided that he wanted to be a dentist.

"So he went to school, got his degree, and later, when I hung out my shingle in Sand Harbor, he did too. He's a good dentist—one of the best. But he drinks too much, and his eyes are bad, from snake poisoning by the way, when he was in Africa. He had done a lot for me and, naturally, I wanted to help him all I could. I send him all the patients I can, and sometimes I even pay his rent.

"He insists upon living alone, and he's got an idea that if he is too friendly with me, it will hurt my practice. Nonsense, of course. But when Bill got sick after using his mouth wash, I was afraid that maybe he had been a little befuddled when he made it up and had included some harmful drug by mistake. Easy to do, you know, especially if your eyes are weak and you've been drinking a little. So I took the mouth wash, to analyze it and make sure it was harmless."

HE STOPPED talking and grinned at me. "We doctors have to stick pretty close together, you know."

"Okay," I said. "I suppose that is why you tried to get away with the stuff the second time?"

"That's right. I was determined to cover up for Doctor Consino, if he needed covering up. A thing like that, if it gets out, can ruin a doctor's career."

Professor Hargrave, followed by George Harker, came into the kitchen.

"He's sleeping now," announced the professor. "The swelling has diminished. The serum is reacting satisfactorily. He'll be fine in a couple of days. Close call, though."

George was smiling, and wiping his glasses with his handkerchief. There was color in his face again.

"Jean, I don't have to tell you how happy I am," he said. "I'm not only going to have you for a daughter-in-law, but I've got a new business partner. From now on it's Harker and Son. Bill says he wants it that way." I wasn't sure, but I thought I saw tears in George's eyes.

"That's fine, George," I said. "Congratulations."

When I looked at George's happy face I felt like the grandfather of all the Judases in the world. But in my business, you never know. I sighed. I was glad that it was McGuire, and not George, who had stopped my slugs out at the garage.

"I feel badly about Gregory," Jean Oliver said. "In some ways, he was kind of nice."

"Yeah," I said. "Nice, like a cobra."

www.ingramcontent.com/pod-product-compliance
Lightning Source LLC
Chambersburg PA
CBHW030538030726
47495CB00004B/1040
9781618276872